LOVE NOTES IN REINDEER FALLS

BETH LABONTE

I've always liked quiet people: You never know if they're dancing in a daydream or if they're carrying the weight of the world.

- John Green, *Looking for Alaska*

CHAPTER 1

I had been racing steadily toward rock bottom when the note arrived. It had come in a plain white envelope, the handwriting shaky and unrecognizable. No return address. I'd toyed with the idea that it was from a secret admirer or a kidnapper. Kidnapper was more likely, the way things had been going. Perhaps Mom and Dad had been taken hostage and this ransom note was their only chance at survival. I had no money with which to pay anybody any sort of ransom, so I'd torn it open with bated breath and hoped for the best.

I saw right away that the note wasn't spelled out with letters cut from the pages of a magazine. Rather, it was from Annabeth Pond, my choir director from back home. Miss Annabeth had taught choir at both the junior high and high school, and had been in charge of the town's annual Christmas show. She was more like family to me, than a teacher, and it was with much guilt that I realized I hadn't spoken with her in a few years. As I read through the note, the words *kidney donor* and *something of great importance to ask* jumped out at me as if they were written in flashing neon, rather than ordinary blue pen.

I'd immediately booked a flight, thrown some clothes into a

suitcase, and told the post office to hold my mail. It was with a passing moment of gloom that I realized I had nobody else to notify. No boyfriend. No close friends who would wonder where I'd gone off to. No job. Like I said, rock bottom coming up fast.

Free as a bird, I flew from Boston, Massachusetts to my tiny hometown of Reindeer Falls, Tennessee. Technically, I flew to Knoxville and drove the rest of the way. Reindeer Falls doesn't exactly have its own airport, unless you want to count the patch of grass in the town square designated as Santa's Landing Strip. Reindeer Falls is certainly unique. One Christmas Eve, way back in the eighteen-hundreds—when the town was simply known as Milford—the mayor had indulged in a bit too much eggnog and claimed to have witnessed a majestic reindeer stepping out from behind the town waterfall. It was all he could talk about for weeks, eventually going so far as re-naming the town so that nobody would ever forget the fact that he'd probably just seen a really big deer. Regardless, the town embraced the idea, and soon just about everything had a Christmas theme.

I was sitting now in Miss Annabeth's cozy living room, waiting while she made a pot of tea. Burl Ives—her plump black cat with the big white paws—was rubbing against my ankles. Burl had been only a kitten the last time I'd seen him, and I enjoyed getting reacquainted while I waited.

Miss Annabeth had sent letters to all three of us—me, Emma, and Michelle—the girls she'd bonded for life with that silly friendship bracelet ritual back in sixth grade. We'd just finished our first ever performance of "I'll Be Home for Christmas" at the community center's Christmas show, and Miss Annabeth had led us all outside into the snow. She said that she'd watched the three of us growing closer over the past few months, and that she wanted to share something with us that she'd once done with her own group of childhood friends.

She pulled three of the woven friendship bracelets that we'd made earlier in the day out of her pocket, and tied one onto each of our wrists. Then, while she read us the old poem that she and her friends had written about friendship being a precious thing, made and woven out of string...we stood there, giggling nervously, but feeling like something truly magical was in the air.

As it turned out, those two girls became my closest friends all throughout junior high and high school. As silly as that bracelet ritual seemed, I've always felt fortunate to have been a part of it—even if we did drift apart after high school. Emma got into modeling and ended up in New York City. Michelle went off to college in California, where she ended up staying. While the three of us still kept in touch by email, it had been a few years since I'd seen either of them in person.

I looked around Miss Annabeth's once immaculate home—now filling up with unwashed dishes, a thick layer of dust on the coffee table, a basket of laundry by the basement door—and I wondered how she was still managing to get by on her own. I suddenly felt guilty that she was in the kitchen making tea for me, a perfectly healthy twenty-six-year-old woman. I stood up and headed toward the kitchen to help, when she appeared in the doorway carrying a tray covered in teacups and cookies.

"Let me take that," I said, gently taking the tray from her hands and setting it on the coffee table. "Sit down." I gingerly put a hand on her shoulder and directed her to the couch. She sat down with a sigh.

"Oh, that's better," she said. "Thank you, dear."

I sat in the wingback chair opposite and looked her over. Shoulder-length silver hair. Minimal wrinkles. She looked tired, and a bit dark beneath her blue eyes, but still elegant. In another life, I always imagined her sweeping about in a Hollywood mansion, sipping martinis and telling stories of her useless ex-husbands, one eye firmly on the pool boy.

"The tea is quite hot," she said. "While we let it cool, would you mind?" She motioned across the living room to the upright piano against the wall.

"Oh," I said, taken aback. "I don't know. It's been so long."

"I'm not asking you to perform at the Grand Ole Opry, dear. Just to play for an old lady in her living room."

I smiled. "Sure, Miss Annabeth."

I walked over and sat nervously down at the piano. I couldn't even remember the last time I had played. I didn't want to make her get up and search for sheet music, so I played the only song that I knew by heart. The theme song from the *Super Mario Bros.* The sound of Miss Annabeth laughing echoed throughout the house as I played, while images of Mario leaping over pipes, fireballs spewing from his hands, flashed through my mind. There were few greater reminders of my childhood. I played the final sad notes as Mario miscalculated a jump and fell to his death, and then I turned around. Miss Annabeth was wiping tears from her eyes.

"Oh, my," she laughed. "I was expecting something dull like 'Moonlight Sonata.' But *that*. That brings back some memories. You girls used to play that game for hours at the community center."

"I know," I said. "That was the whole reason I hung out there. Mom and Dad wouldn't buy me video games. I did, however, have a hoop and a stick." I walked over and sat down next to her on the couch. She brushed a stray piece of my long, auburn hair over my shoulder, her hand cold as it brushed against my cheek.

"Beautiful girl," she said. "You've always been able to make me laugh."

I smiled, happy to have brought a few minutes of joy to Miss Annabeth, although I sensed that the conversation was about to take a serious turn.

"But now we do need to get down to business," she continued. "The reason I asked all of you girls to come home is because I have a small favor to ask."

"Of course. You need a kidney."

Miss Annabeth looked at me as if I'd totally lost my mind. "Good lord, no!"

"What do you mean *no?* You need one, don't you?"

"Well, *yes*. But I would never ask for one from you girls." She took a sip of tea, a bit angrily. "I'm on the donor list, Caitlin, and that's that. That part of it is none of your concern."

I sank back into the couch, somewhat let down. Somewhat relieved. Somewhat ticked off that I'd blown my rent money on a plane ticket...for what?

"What is it that you need, then?" I asked slowly, through gritted teeth.

"My request is much simpler than that," she sighed. "All I want is for you girls to perform again at the Christmas show. You've drifted much too far apart lately. The friendship bonds you formed that special night have become much too loose over the years. You do remember the bracelets, don't you?" She looked at me accusingly, one eyebrow raised. I glanced down at my bare wrist and nodded guiltily.

"Well," she continued, "it would give me great peace to know that you girls are going to be there for each other after...after I'm gone." Her voice broke slightly. "In fact, it would make the entire town happy to see you girls together again."

The Christmas show had always been quite the event in our tiny town. After that first performance of "I'll Be Home for Christmas"—with me on piano and the other girls singing—the three of us decided to turn it into an annual tradition. The town loved it. After our final performance, right before we'd graduated from high school and gone our separate ways, the *Reindeer Falls Gazette* had even printed an article lamenting the end of an era.

We were sort of a big deal.

But as much as I wanted to give Miss Annabeth peace of mind, I would rather walk through Harvard Square in my graduation cap and underwear than play the piano in front of such a large audience again. Sure, I could play a decent rendition of the

Super Mario Bros. theme, but I hadn't actually sat down and practiced in forever. Over the past eight years, music had taken a back
seat to everything else in my life.

"Have the other girls agreed to do it?" I asked.

"You're the first one who's been kind enough to come see me,
Caity," she said, taking a small sip of tea, her eyes shifting toward
the floor. "But when they do come, if I could tell them that *you'd*
already agreed to it, well…"

I loved Miss Annabeth, but she could be a manipulative little
bugger when she wanted. She once reverse-psychologied me into
agreeing to accompany the Reindeer Falls Men's Club's performance of *Show Boat*. That was in tenth grade, and I still haven't
quite forgiven her. But, for the most part, she was a sweetheart.

"You know I never could say no to you," I sighed. "So, yes. For
you, Miss Annabeth, I'll do it."

"Wonderful!" she said, reaching over and squeezing my hand.
"I'm so glad."

As soon as I saw that familiar sparkle return to her eyes, I
knew I'd made the right decision.

"There *is* one more thing," she added. "I didn't want to
mention it in the letter, on top of everything else, but the town
just doesn't have the money to keep the community center open
much longer. After this year's Christmas show, they're planning
to close it down."

"Oh, no," I said, frowning. "Isn't there anything we can do?"

"We've done some fundraising," she said, nodding thoughtfully. "That's how we've managed to stay open as long as we have.
But there are only so many boxes of cookies and rolls of wrapping paper we can sell. Especially with money being so tight for
everybody around here."

My shoulders slumped. Everything truly seemed to be falling
apart all at once. First my boyfriend, then my job. Now the
community center, where I'd forged my closest childhood friendships, was going to be nothing but a rundown empty shell the

next time I came back to Reindeer Falls. Worst of all was the thought of Miss Annabeth no longer being with us. Tears stung my eyes as the sad reality sank in.

"We'll figure something out," I said. "I promise. And you'll get that kidney donor. Just relax and try to stay positive. If there's one place destined for a Christmas miracle, it's a town called Reindeer Falls."

"That is true," she said, patting my hand and taking a sip of tea. "Thank goodness we're not still called Milford."

CHAPTER 2

*M*y bed was in there somewhere. It had to be. Mom had told me over the phone, just last week, that all my things were still where I'd left them. She'd also said that I was welcome to come home at any time—didn't I *know* that I never needed to ask? —and that there would be a Christmas tree, a home-cooked meal, and a warm bed waiting for me. Only, standing in the doorway of my childhood bedroom, gazing into the overflowing abyss of Amazon shipping boxes, knickknacks, clothing, stuffed animals, books, and who knew what else, there wasn't a warm bed in sight. The home-cooked meal was also starting to seem unlikely.

Unless...

There was a large, vaguely rectangular mound in the corner of the room. My eyes followed the gentle sloping of clutter that rose up from the floor and ended just below the window. I stepped carefully into the room, parkouring my way across the various items, trying my best to avoid stepping too heavily in any one spot. Something hard crunched beneath my heel. I hoped there weren't any pets hiding in here. Our family cat, Pickles, had passed away years ago and as far as I knew, Mom and Dad had never gotten a replacement. The last thing I needed was to hear a crunch and a meow as I put down my foot.

With a leap, and a mercifully meowless landing, I made it to the corner of the room. I tossed a huge pile of clothing off the rectangular mound, revealing the pink and orange patchwork of my teenaged bedspread. I could only see a few square inches of it, but it was definitely there. Mom hadn't been lying. Which meant that the rest of my stuff was also still there. Just...buried.

I sank down onto the bed, a life raft amongst the hoard, and surveyed my room from this new angle. Mom and Dad may have turned the floor space of my bedroom into a chaotic catchall, but anything I had hung from the walls had managed to stay intact. A homemade photo collage still hung over the bureau, the faces of my two best friends smiling back at me. Bracelet Buddies forever. We were surrounded by colorful words cut from magazines: *Remember the Times! Besties!* I wondered how many of my old friends had returned home to find similar reminders of their youth. Probably just me. Normal parents would have packed up all this junk years ago. Normal parents would have thrown it all away once their child had moved out.

It had been two years since I'd been home—and yes, I cringed after I'd worked out the calculations. Visiting me on the East Coast was always the more exciting option for Mom, Dad, and my little brother Nate, so it had always been easy for me to avoid coming home to Tennessee. As for the holidays, I spent last Christmas and this past Thanksgiving with my ex-boyfriend Ben's wealthy family up in cozy, picturesque Vermont. He took me on a sleigh ride with horses, and jingle bells, and right on cue, a dusting of snow had swirled down from the sky. It was legit holiday magic and I'd arrived back in Boston with the sense that all was right with the world.

Two days later, a love note written by one of Ben's female coworkers fell into my lap. I'd been happily watching a rerun of *Twin Peaks,* lost in the Douglas firs and cherry pie, when Ben came in, stood next to the couch, and the note literally fell out of his pocket and into my lap. Legit holiday magic over. Three days later I lost my job. The thought of returning home for Christmas, single and unemployed, made it a bit hard to breathe. That was, until Miss Annabeth's note arrived and the decision was made for me.

Growing up in the Cook household, things had always been somewhat cramped and hard to breathe. Various pieces of furniture that Mom and Dad planned to restore and sell in their antique shop, Christmas Past, were always found around the house. Rocking chair in the bathroom. Floor to ceiling mirror wedged beside the refrigerator. There was a period of time when we ate all of our meals around a pair of wooden skis. For most of my childhood, it was quirky and fun. It had been manageable. Junk came in, and junk went out. It was my parents' livelihood and it had worked. But as the years went on, there came a noticeable turning of the tides where the junk came in, but it didn't always go out. What had once been quirky and fun had started giving me anxiety and claustrophobia.

You used to not be able to tell from the outside of the house what was happening on the inside. Driving down our rural road, our big white farmhouse with the black shutters looked just like any other. Sure, it was a little shabby and a little rustic—but it mostly looked homey and lived in. But as soon as I pulled into the driveway after two years away, I noticed the difference immediately. Things that didn't belong outside had begun creeping onto the porch. An old recliner. A rowing machine. An outdated, boxy computer monitor covered in spider webs and leaves. On closer inspection, I saw that it was *my* computer monitor. The one I had typed all my high school papers on. My first reaction was to feel sorry for it. What was once a state-of-the-art piece of computing equipment, integral to my education, had been abandoned to the outdoors to become a housing development for mice. My second reaction, felt deep in the pit of my stomach, was dread. Because the only reason a computer monitor would be out on the front porch, was if there just wasn't enough room for it anywhere else.

The sound of a key in the lock downstairs pulled me quickly back to the present.

"Caity?" shouted Mom. "Are you here?"

"Coming!" I jumped off the bed and made my way down the stairs. My heart was suddenly bursting with excitement at the thought of seeing my family.

"Sweetheart!" said Mom. She stepped deftly around various piles of things, using a path that only she could see, and swept me into a hug.

"Hi, Mom," I said into her neck. Same old Mom. Dressed in a thick wool cardigan and smelling like a flea market.

"Hi, Dad," I said, tripping over a pile of extension cords as I went to him for a hug. Same old Dad. Dressed like a flea market and smelling like a thick wool cardigan. I'd missed them both.

"Nathan," I said, stepping back and gently punching my brother on the shoulder. To my surprise, he stepped forward to give me a hug. Nate was sixteen, and I felt a wave of concern due to the fact that he has *never* wanted to hug me.

"It's good to see you," he mumbled.

Or said that it was good to see me.

"It's good to see you, too." I took a step back and looked up into his face. He was taller than me now, and a bit gangly. He was quickly becoming a miniature version of Dad, minus the mustache. "How are you?"

"I spent the morning at an estate sale with Mom and Dad. How do you think I am?" On that note, he loped off toward the stairs, using the same path over the junk as had Mom. I still couldn't see it.

"Estate sale?" I looked from Mom to Dad and back again. "How'd that go?" I didn't see anybody carrying any plastic Thank You bags, which was a good sign. There seemed to be more than

11

enough stuff already in the house—never mind what they prob-ably had at the store—to keep them in business for the next twenty years.

"It's all out in the truck," said Dad, grinning.

"All?" My eyes widened. "*Truck?*" Mom and Dad didn't own a truck, as far as I knew.

Mom put her arm lovingly around Dad's shoulders and gave him a shake. "This one just had to have Giles Wilson's International Harvester. He's had his eye on it for years. Giles finally sold it to him for three grand. Said he needed the money to pay medical bills and your father, the old ghoul, he jumped at the chance."

"I tried to offer him five!" protested Dad, throwing his hands out in front of him. "But he wouldn't hear of it!"

"Go have a look," said Mom, motioning to the front door.

I stared at them both for a moment—they looked as if they had just brought their third child into the world—before making my way to the door. Mater from *Cars* was parked in the drive-way, minus the buckteeth. The truck was painted a rusty shade of red, with retro aqua hubcaps, and the words "Wilson's Feed Store" still stenciled on the side in white lettering. The back was piled high with a heap of old furniture, and I stifled a giggle at the thought of the three of them stuffed into the front seat, bouncing on home like the Beverly Hillbillies. Poor Nate.

"Dining set, armoire, boxes full of jewelry. Esther Adams passed away last month. Ninety-seven years old. Her daughter's selling everything," said Dad, in his clipped way of speaking. He joined me by the door. "No choice sometimes. Folks are having a rough time around here. Especially this time of year."

I looked up at Dad in concern. Miss Annabeth had also mentioned money being tight lately, but my parents had never mentioned money troubles to me before. Our family had always lived simply, and with the tourism spillover from Gatlinburg, they'd always had a fairly steady stream of business.

"Your mom and I are hanging in there," he added, giving me a reassuring squeeze around the shoulders. "We're hanging in there. You might even say we've been reaping the benefits!" He nodded toward Giles Wilson's truck filled with Esther Adams' worldly possessions.

"He's a ghoul!" shouted Mom from the living room.

Dad chuckled as he headed outside to unload the truck.

"So, Mom," I said, joining her in the living room. "Things have changed a bit since I've last been here." I gestured from the couch, where there wasn't a single place to sit, to the stack of boxes obscuring the picture window.

"Oh," said Mom, looking vaguely around, her eyes skimming over objects her brain had filtered out. "I suppose the place could use some tidying up. We're just so busy doing restorations and school things with Nate..."

"And a tree! Mom, there's no Christmas tree!"

"It's still early. We'll get one."

"You promised me a tree." I made a mopey little girl face.

"We'll *get* one, Caity. We just need to...clear a space." She looked optimistically toward the corner where we'd always displayed our tree. It was presently occupied by a fortress of boxes marked *Doll Heads.*

"Come on," said Mom, steering me out of the living room and changing the subject. "I'll make you some coffee and we can catch up before the concert!"

The annual holiday band concert was being held tonight at the high school. Nate played the trumpet. I knew it was just a lame high school concert, but I was still pretty excited to go. I had performed in it every year that I was in high school. I was a flute player, as well as the piano accompanist for the choir and jazz band. I was sure they'd be playing all the same arrangements of all the same holiday songs that I remembered. Everybody would be dressed in the same uniform of black pants, white shirts, and red bow ties. There would be holiday decorations and a table of baked goods for sale by the music boosters.

There would also be Shane.

"You know who the band director is now, don't you?" asked Mom, reading my mind as she moved things around, attempting to locate the coffeemaker. I watched as she pulled a box of K-Cups out of the microwave.

"Um, yep."

"Shane Mitchell!" she exclaimed. My response was clearly not dismissive enough. She suddenly stopped what she was doing and turned to look at me, her face bearing the same expression of scrunched-up concern as when I told her I had chosen Harvard over Vanderbilt. "You know, I didn't even think that it might be awkward for you, seeing him again."

"It's no big deal, Mom. He'll be with the band. He probably won't even notice me. Besides, we've kept in touch on Facebook."

By "we've kept in touch on Facebook," I meant that I'd stared at all his public photos without having the nerve to send him a friend request. I certainly didn't want to run into him at the concert, but there was no easy way to avoid going. Nate had a trumpet solo and it would hurt his feelings if I skipped. Besides, I was more nostalgic for my band days than I was nervous about bumping into Shane. The odds were slim.

"I never did get into that Facebook stuff," muttered Mom, fishing around in a metal tin, pulling out receipts, coupons, and finally a handful of sugar packets.

Probably because the computer's out on the front porch, I thought, taking a few sugar packets and finding myself a spot at the kitchen island. I rested my coffee mug in the space between a pair of antique snowshoes.

"You working on fixing these up?" I asked.

Mom looked down at the snowshoes with a furrowed brow. She had clearly stopped noticing they were there ages ago.

"Eventually," she said, with a dismissive wave. "So, tell me,

Caity, what's this all about? Coming home like this out of the blue? Not that I'm not grateful. I'm thrilled to have you home. We all are. This past Christmas and Thanksgiving just weren't the same."

"I know, Mom," I said, my chest filling with regret. "I'm sorry about that. And this year, well"—I paused to take a sip of coffee— "to be honest, I didn't think I'd have the money for a plane ticket."

"They're paying you at that job of yours, aren't they? Please don't tell me it's another unpaid internship."

"I had *one* unpaid internship, Mom. And that was four years ago. Of course, they pay me now. How do you think I've been surviving on my own all these years?"

Mom just shrugged. "Well then, what happened?"

I sighed. "Three days after Ben and I broke up, I lost my job."

"Oh, no," she said. "I'm so sorry."

"It's not like publishing history books was my dream job," I said, shrugging. "I'll find something else. Anyway, even if I had the money to fly home, I was embarrassed to show up here single and unemployed. I was considering making something up about going to Vermont again. I almost told you that Ben and I had gotten back together."

"That boy *does not* deserve a second chance." Mom's concerned face was back with a vengeance, moments away from calling my father into the house for an intervention.

"It was a lie, Mom. Remember?"

"Right. Good." She put down the napkin she'd been twisting between her fingers and her face lit up. "Does this mean you're moving back home?"

I ignored the question. "That's when I got the note in the mail from Miss Annabeth. She told me that she needs a kidney transplant." I fought back tears as I said the words out loud. "She's asked Michelle, Emma, and me to perform again at the Christmas show. She wants to see it again, just in case this is her last chance."

15

"Oh, Caity," said Mom, putting one hand over her mouth. "I had no idea."

"She doesn't want anybody to feel sorry for her," I sighed. "But she really is sick. And not only that, the community center is running out of money. She told me that after the Christmas show, the town is closing it down."

Mom patted my hand and shook her head in sympathy.

"Anyway," I continued. "As soon as I got her note, I packed my bags, used the last of my rent money to buy a plane ticket, and here I am!" I threw my hands in the air.

Mom took a sip of coffee, but I could tell by her eyes that she was smiling behind her mug.

"You have some nerve calling *Dad* an old ghoul," I said. "Tell me, Mom, what part of my favorite teacher being ill, me losing my job, my boyfriend, and my childhood memories, are you smiling about?"

"Don't be morbid, love. I'm not happy about any of that."

"Then what is it?"

"I'll let you in on a little secret," she said. "Even if you were here because the entire East Coast had fallen into the ocean"— she reached across the counter and squeezed me by the wrists— "I'd still be happy to see my daughter."

"Thanks, Mom." I smiled back. Then a thought occurred to me. "Do you think that if the entire East Coast *were* to fall into the ocean, my student loans would be forgiven?"

Mom shrugged and took another sip of coffee. "Never give up hope, love." She motioned toward the front of the house. "That's how your father got his truck."

CHAPTER 3

*W*alking into my high school felt like a dream—like some sort of Lynchian convoluted fantasy sequence where everything looked familiar, yet everything looked completely *wrong*. Maybe I was being a bit dramatic. Maybe I'd spent the entire flight from Boston to Tennessee re-watching episodes of *Twin Peaks*. Still, it was impossible to deny that there were subtle changes everywhere I looked. Security cameras had been installed in the lobby. The walls had been repainted from their infamous shade of vomit green to a more neutral cream, which I found somewhat disappointing. Even the lighting was different, though I wasn't quite sure how. Had Reindeer Falls High School gone energy efficient? Bizarre. I wondered briefly if they'd fixed the feminine hygiene receptacle in the first-floor girls' room—the one you could stick your hand through and wave to your friend in the next stall.

A few changes might be for the better.

I told Mom and Dad that I would meet them in the auditorium, and wandered away to have a closer look at the wall of framed senior photos. I walked down the row of frames until I found my graduating class. Our school had always kept the past

ten years' worth of photos up on the wall, so mine was still there
—inching closer to the end, but not yet gone. Not yet bubble-
wrapped and boxed and put into storage alongside the out-of-
date textbooks and broken music stands. Not that I could picture
our crotchety old custodian, Mr. Wexler, fondly packaging up old
student photographs. More likely, he torched each one while
reading from an itemized list of messes he had been forced to
clean on our behalf. No way had Mr. Wexler retired. He was way
too angry of a human to sit around the house doing crosswords.
It was possible that he was dead. Even then, I liked to imagine
him floating up and down the corridors, grumbling *Chicken
patties in the TOILET?* under his ghostly breath.

I ran my finger along the bottom of the frame, wincing as I
located my senior portrait. I had posed with my flute. My *flute.*
What kind of a dork poses with her flute? As if that weren't bad
enough, I had it resting across my chest like a musket—as if I had
just enlisted in the Confederate Army, only not nearly as cool. To
top it off, rather than looking at the camera, I was gazing lovingly
down its silvery shaft. I suddenly wished Mr. Wexler were there,
armed with his blowtorch. I'd have paid good money to watch
that photo turn to ashes. I continued along the little squares of
photos, stopping in the second row, third from the left. Blue
shirt, striped tie, dirty blond hair neatly combed, just waiting for
the okay to be tousled. A smile that said, *as soon as I leave this
studio, I'm going to do something I'll regret.* How this photo could be
the same one I had carried around in my wallet that first year of
college, I had no idea. I'd thought we were adults.

When Shane Mitchell stood in front of me, the night before I
left for Harvard, telling me that he loved me, I thought I had been
looking at a man. When I spent my entire freshman year awash
in regrets and what ifs, I thought that I had made the biggest
mistake of my life. My *adult* life.

But as I reached up and gently touched the glass over his
frozen, teenaged face, the reality of just how totally wrong I was

hit me like a shovel. He was a *baby*. We both were. Shane wasn't much older than Nate in that photo, and Nate and his friends were probably goofing around backstage giving each other wedgies. If Nate ever told me that he was in love I'd probably laugh in his face. Not because I was mean, but because life hadn't even begun to happen for him yet. To think you knew anything about love at that age was ludicrous.

"It's a handsome picture, I'll admit. But I always thought my Glamour Shots came out better."

I froze at the sound of the voice behind me, and then slowly withdrew my hand from the glass.

"Don't be embarrassed," it continued. "I blow yours a kiss every morning when I walk by. Funny thing is, I can't seem to compete with that look you've been giving your flute."

I bit my bottom lip to keep from laughing, and turned slowly around. The baby-faced teenager who was lingering in my mind faded away, replaced by the grown man now standing in front of me. His dirty blond hair was shorter than I remembered, and neatly combed for the occasion. It was only a matter of time before he raked his fingers through it. He was probably itching to do it right then, using his nervous energy to instead roll up the sleeves of his white dress shirt. Self-control had never been his strong suit. Still, everything about him was more mature. More filled out. Even that familiar smile resided above a more angular jaw, topped off by a pair of sky-blue eyes. Those same eyes had spent four years making me sweat, then eight more filling me with regret.

Everything the same, but everything different.

"Shane," I said.

"Caitlin Cook. It's been a while."

My eyes flicked from his face down to his surfing Santa Claus necktie.

"Nice tie."

"It plays a song. Want to try?" He pointed to the middle of his chest where, if I were completely deranged, I might walk over and press my fingers.

"No. And for the record, I wasn't looking at your picture."

"Don't lie to me, Caity. I could tell by the wistful gaze and the sparkle in your eye."

"I was facing the wall."

"I can read the back of your head like a book."

"So, you've learned to read?"

We stood in silence for a few moments, assessing each other. Trying to remember where we had left things off, and determining where exactly to pick things up. I had painfully vivid memories of the former. No clue about the latter. How was he being so darn nonchalant? He had blindsided me completely back then. And when I'd come back home for that very first Christmas break, confident in my decision to go ahead and take the plunge, aglow in the realization that I was, in fact, in love with Shane—he had already moved on with someone else.

"So, how are you?" I asked at last. I took a hesitant step forward, as if going in for a hug, before coming to my senses and pulling back. The result being an awkward little curtsy bob. Shoot me.

With an amused smile, Shane mirrored my awkward curtsy bob, and time rewound. We were eighteen again, and it was the summer after senior year. Time wasn't just running out, time was gone. Game over. My bags were packed. I was bound for Boston and Shane was suddenly in love. Who did he think he *was*? A burning heat started rising in my chest, which was a feeling that Shane's Facebook photos had never managed to invoke. Maybe Mom was right. Maybe coming here was a bad idea. Of *course,* I was going to run into him. Then again, maybe I knew that all along.

"I'm good," he said. "How are you?"

"Good," I answered, stiffly. "Great."

"It's been what? Six, seven years?"

"Eight."

Shane gave me a wink. "I see you've been counting. Or should I say, pining?"

I rolled my eyes. "It's simple math, dummy."

"We didn't all go to Harvard," said Shane. "I've only been back a couple of years myself. I'd been teaching music down in Georgia, then Mom and Dad decided to retire to Florida. Now I own their house."

"Oh, wow," I said, impressed. "Just you? Or did you have to move your, um, your whole family?"

"My Uncle Roger's pretty happy where he is in Chattanooga."

I gave him a death stare, but he didn't budge. I didn't press the issue. The lack of a wedding band on his finger was all the answer I needed.

We were interrupted by a few parents stopping by to shake hands with Shane, calling him "Mr. M" and congratulating him on a great marching band season. I raised my eyebrows after they'd gone.

"*Mr. M,* huh? You're like a local celebrity. Look out Matthew McConaughey!" I waved my hands mockingly in the air, followed by an unexpected snort of laughter, followed by a fake cough as I tried to cover it up. No wonder I had posed with my flute. I wasn't cool. Never had been.

"I wouldn't go that far," said Shane, stepping closer to pat me on the back. "You okay?"

"Fine!" The touch of his hand went through me like a jolt of electricity. I reacted by pushing him away, which set off a tinny rendition of "Deck the Halls" from his necktie. It was all too much and we both started to laugh.

"So, big, serious Mr. M." I air-quoted the name, once I'd pulled myself together. "Do those kids in there have any idea what you used to be like?"

"And what exactly did I used to be like?" asked Shane, fixing me with a loaded half smile.

My stomach flipped. What word to use? Spastic? Perplexing? Diabolical?

In my mind we were eighteen again. Seventeen. Sixteen. *Fifteen*. A fifteen-year-old Shane, sauntering like clockwork up the aisle of the bus, leaving behind whichever girl he'd been sitting with. Flopping into the seat beside me because he was bored. Every band trip. Always. Then would come the questions. Increasingly personal and highly inappropriate, he would pepper me with them, while I ignored him and pretended to read. The more intellectual the book, the dumber the questions. Eventually I would break, bursting into laughter. Then it was my turn. Mortifying questions until I made him laugh. Neither of us ever answered a single one.

By senior year I had a notebook full of them under my bed, jotting them down as they came to me while I did my homework. I always liked to be prepared. A few times I succeeded in making him blush, though that didn't count as a win. Laughter was always the goal, and as soon as he had remedied his boredom, he was gone again to the back of the bus. Back to whichever girl he had left stewing in her seat, shooting daggers into the back of my head.

"Mr. M!" We were mercifully interrupted by Nate and several other boys poking their heads out of the auditorium. "We're ready for warm-up."

"Be right there," said Shane. He gave me an apologetic smile and started backing toward the auditorium door. "I'm sorry. I didn't realize what time it was."

"Of course," I said, relieved. "My parents are probably wondering what happened to me. I'll see you around, Shane."

With a hesitant smile, he turned around, walked a few steps, then stopped and turned around again.

"How about tomorrow?"

"Huh?"

"How about you see me around tomorrow? I'll buy you a coffee and we can finish catching up."

"Sure," I said. "That'd be nice." Or awkward, and painful, and pretty much the worst. Unfortunately, people don't say those things in polite society.

"Great. Three o'clock? Meet me at Holly's?"

"Perfect," I replied, my throat dry. The thought of the two of us alone at a coffee shop was making the room spin.

"I'll see you then." Shane headed toward the auditorium, but stopped again once he'd reached the door. "Hey, do you remember that game we used to play?"

"What game?" I crinkled up my nose as if I really wasn't sure.

"Questions?"

"Yeah. Questions." He looked dreamily off into the distance for a moment, raking his fingers through his neatly combed hair. Then he focused his gaze back on me. "Prepare yourself, Cook. I've been working on some doozies."

With a wink, he disappeared into the auditorium for warm-up.

CHAPTER 4

$\mathcal{T}$he beauty of having hoarders for parents is that, as promised, everything was right where I'd left it. Not convenient to get at, mind you. But there.

I was flat on my stomach the next morning, peering underneath my bed, looking for that notebook. If we were going to be playing Questions at three o'clock, I was going to be prepared. Years' worth of stuff that my parents dumped onto the bedroom floor had been swept underneath the bed like one of those coin-pusher games at the arcade. With a broom in one hand, I reached into the depths and started knocking things out. Bundles of unopened junk mail, magazines, cat toys. The thought that my next sweep might pull out poor Pickles himself briefly crossed my mind. Every clump of dust bunnies had me doing a double take.

Eventually, the junk started giving way to items that I recognized. Pink flip-flop. Sheet music. Plastic box full of notes folded into neat little footballs. Those were the notes my friends and I had passed each other between classes. I couldn't believe I'd left such personal stuff here. At least it was obvious that Mom and Dad had never looked at any of it. Finally, I saw it—the pink plastic spiral binding, with a black and white chevron cover. I pinned it with the broom and yanked it toward me. Dusting it off, I leaned back against the side of the bed and opened the cover.

Oh.

Oh, *my*.

I knew Shane and I had asked each other embarrassing questions—that was the whole point of the game—but this notebook was a whole other level of depravity. I clamped a hand over my mouth, hardly believing the things I had written. Holy cow. No wonder Shane had ditched his girlfriends to come and sit with me. I had the grace of a filthy sailor. I guess it's true what they say about it *always being the quiet ones*. Jaw still dropped, I slammed the notebook shut. Did I actually ask him that stuff? A small bit of hope swelled up inside me. Maybe I had just jotted those ideas down, but never actually used them. Like, a first draft. I opened the notebook to a random page. Nope. I definitely remembered asking him *that* one. I could even picture the exact look on his face when I'd said it. Oh, and that one, too. That one had gotten quite the chuckle. I felt the heat rising in my cheeks.

So, okay. Probably not a good idea to bring up these questions over coffee today. Not even for a laugh. There wasn't even anything that funny about them now that we were adults. Besides, it was because of those stupid questions that Shane thought he had somehow fallen in love with me. *Me.* The shy girl, always with her nose in a book, whom he liked to pester on the bus. And it was thanks to those stupid questions that I had spent four years crushing on a big, fat, blue-eyed pie in the sky. Freshman year was the very first time he'd flopped into the seat next to me with his very first question: *Why are you so quiet?* How I loathed that question. How I had loathed *him* for asking it. There was no good answer for it, so I didn't give one. Instead, I asked a question of my own: *Why are you so lame?* He'd thought that was hilarious, as if I were the first person to ever string those five words together, and so it all began.

I tossed the notebook into the plastic box of folded notes and placed the whole thing on my desk. I was alone in the house. Nate was at school and Mom and Dad were at the shop. I was planning to stop by that afternoon, after meeting Shane for coffee, to see how business was doing. Christmas Past and Holly's were on opposite ends of Main Street, but still only about a three-minute walk from each other. The coziness of Reindeer Falls, after living in a city of half a million people, never ceased to amaze me.

I walked out of my bedroom and down the hall. Nate's bedroom door was closed, but that didn't stop me. I pushed it open and peered inside, wondering for a moment if I had the wrong room. Had Nate moved into the basement? All I could see were stacks of cardboard boxes, four or five high, lining the left-hand wall. As I stepped all the way into the room, I spotted Nate's Star Wars bedspread laid across an unmade twin-sized bed. A laptop was on the desk under the window. Typical teenaged boy posters lined the walls. This was still his room. And apparently, he was really into Selena Gomez.

I walked over to the first column of boxes and lifted the lid. It was filled with antique photos of nineteenth-century theater actresses. Unless Nate's taste in girls had recently taken an odd turn, these boxes belonged to Mom and Dad. I walked over to the closet and opened the door. Nate's shirts hung from the hangers in disarray, while the floor was taken up by an assortment of antique butter churns. For Pete's sake.

I had assumed Mom and Dad were using my room for storage because I no longer lived at home. But *Nate*? He was still living there! He deserved his own space. He *needed* his own space. Could he even have friends over? I pictured Mom and Dad tromping in and out of his room to get at their things, asking him to relocate his stuff so they could pile up their newly acquired farm equipment. With a frown I closed the closet door. I was going to have to have a talk with Mom and Dad.

I hadn't yet thought of a Christmas present for Nate, but I was starting to get an idea of what he might desperately need.

* * *

WITH NOTHING else to do that afternoon, I decided to spend a few hours poking around Reindeer Falls before meeting Shane. I parked my rental car beside Santa's Landing Strip—Giles Wilson had already decked it out with super classy red and green blinking lights—and walked past it toward the center of the town square. I came to a stop in front of the life-sized bronze reindeer that had been erected, long ago, in honor of our town's name-sake. Somebody had hung a large wreath around his neck, and there was a bit of bird poop on one of his antlers.

"Hey there, Clip-Clop," I said, stuffing my hands into my pockets and looking up into his long face. Clip-Clop wasn't his official name or anything. It was just what I'd nicknamed him when I was five. It was the sound I imagined his hooves made on Christmas Eve, when he came to life and trotted down Main Street. Because, *obviously,* that's what he did. I closed my eyes for a moment, and listened to the faint sound of the Falls in the distance. I opened my eyes and looked across the town square to the community center. Somebody had hung a wreath on the front door, but it was lopsided, and one of the front windows had been broken. Behind it—with an amazing view of the Falls—was the Heavenly Peace Senior Living Community. I'd always found the name of that place incredibly funny. It sounded more like a funeral home than a home for the living. But from where I stood, I could see a group of elderly people outside in the sun, either doing Zumba or being chased by bees. Good for them.

I said goodbye to Clip-Clop and jogged across the town square to Main Street, slowing down and taking my time as I walked up the sidewalk. There was Mad Dasher's Mini Mart on the right, with its window full of lottery announcements. A faded, controversial ad showing Dasher smoking a pack of Camels, was still posted in the lower corner. I could see Cliff Clemson inside behind the counter, still bearded and burly. His older brother, Rudy, ran a Christmas tree farm in town, and was always the friendlier of the two.

My parents' antique shop was across the street, its windows jammed with vintage Christmas decorations and outlined with red tinsel and white twinkling lights. I caught a glimpse of Dad climbing up his rickety old step-ladder that had belonged to Grandpa, and said a prayer that he not fall and kill himself. A bit further up was The Greasy Antler, with its red vinyl booths visible through the front window. If you could get past the name, it really was the best place to eat. Inside, Tammy Pulaski—who'd been working there since Mom and Dad were in high school—was taking somebody's order.

Each of the lampposts along the sidewalk had been adorned with a large wreath and a bow. And while they hadn't been turned on yet, I could see strands of lights wrapped around the branches of each maple tree. It was while I was staring dopily up at the trees that a familiar voice called out my name.

"Caitlin?"

I looked toward the entrance of Nick's General Store, my eyes lighting up when I realized who it was.

"Michelle!" I exclaimed, walking over and throwing my arms around my old friend. She hugged me back.

"I was going to text you as soon as I got settled," she said, after we'd let go of each other. "I only flew in a few hours ago and real-ized I'd forgotten a few things." She jerked her head toward Nick's, her long, dark waves bouncing.

"Miss Annabeth's letter had you packing in a hurry too, huh?"

She nodded. "I was planning on coming home for Christmas anyway. My grandparents are moving into Heavenly Peace, and I wanted to be around to help them pack. But that wasn't supposed to be for a few more weeks. Then I got that letter and I didn't want to waste any more time. I'm heading over to see Miss Annabeth right now. Have you been yet?"

"I stopped by yesterday," I said. "She looks okay, but really tired. And her house is a mess. She doesn't seem to have anyone helping her with laundry or cleaning. She didn't have a single Christmas decoration up, either."

Michelle frowned. "When I saw her last Christmas, the inside of her house was all decked out."

"At least you saw her last Christmas," I said, filling with shame.

"Well, we're both here now," said Michelle, always the most motherly of the three of us. "We'll take care of her. Maybe I'll pop back into Nick's and grab a few decorations. I think I saw some of those battery-powered twinkle lights on sale. She'll like those."

"That's a good idea," I said, smiling. "I'll come with you and get her a few things myself."

We walked back into Nick's and cheerfully started tossing the brightest items we could find into our baskets.

"So, what's new with you?" I asked, holding up a plush reindeer wearing a Speedo. Michelle grabbed it out of my hand and tossed it into her basket. The last time we'd talked, she'd been living in San Francisco and working two jobs—as an activities coordinator at a nursing home, and recording audiobooks from her home studio. Michelle had a great speaking voice. "Are you still seeing...Darren, was it?"

"Baron," she corrected, rolling her eyes. "And no."

"I'm sorry."

She shrugged. "Expensive jewelry can only make up for lack of personality for so long. How about you? Still seeing Ben? Still in the coma-inducing world of text book publication?"

"No and no. I actually need to start job hunting as soon as I get back to Boston."

29

"How about man hunting?"

"Not currently on the agenda." An image of Shane running his hand through his hair flashed through my mind. "Still working two jobs?"

"Sure am. I just signed on to narrate a ten-book series of billionaire romances. My rent's going up though, so even with the two jobs, I'll probably have to find a new place to live…which also means the joy of setting up a new recording space again."

"Have you thought about buying a place out there?"

She snorted. "Only if I can find myself one of those billionaires. They're so plentiful on Amazon, aren't they? In real life… not so much." She picked up a box of chocolate reindeer poop, then put it down again. "Anyway, I still don't even know if I want to settle down permanently in California. With my grandparents moving and putting their house up for sale, it's giving me a lot to think about. You ever think about moving back here?"

"I have a life back in Boston," I lied. "I couldn't just pack up and move." The truth was, I had no life and totally could. But when I thought about the hoard of stuff that was taking over my parents' house, I felt the urge to flee the state, not move back home.

After we'd finished shopping for Miss Annabeth, Michelle and I made plans to get together again soon with Emma. We would also have to get together at least once to rehearse before the show.

"Do you remember, oh, when was it? Sophomore year?" she asked. "When part of the roof collapsed in the middle of our song?"

"Yes!" I laughed, holding the door open for old Dottie Cross, who had taught my entire family at Reindeer Falls High, but didn't seem to recognize me. "Thank goodness nobody was hurt. Giles hadn't bothered to clear off the snow and the roof couldn't take the weight."

"Miss Annabeth really let him have it. I'll never forget the

30

words I heard come out of that sweet woman's mouth. And on Christmas Day!"

"Then you and Emma finished the song outside in the parking lot."

"To the sound of police sirens."

We laughed and reminisced for a few more minutes, before Michelle checked her watch and realized that she needed to get going.

"It was so good to see you again," I said, hugging her goodbye. And it really was. It had been much too long since I'd spent time with someone who knew me the way Michelle did. Just from our short time together at Nick's, I spent the rest of the afternoon with a happy buzz of adrenaline. Although, as it grew closer to the time I was supposed to meet Shane for coffee, the feeling started to fade. And by the time three o'clock rolled around, I was sick to my stomach with nerves.

CHAPTER 5

I saw him from across the street, sitting in the window of Holly's, wearing a black coat and scrolling through his phone. I couldn't see his legs, but I was fairly certain they were jiggling with nervous energy. The only time they weren't was when he was playing the piano or the drums. I walked through the door, and at the sound of the bells, he looked up and smiled. He came over to meet me by the door, raking his fingers through his hair as he went. This time we greeted each other with a hug. Between the Christmas music, the smell of coffee and cinnamon in the air, and the wonder of Shane Mitchell suddenly being in my arms, I found myself a bit overcome with emotion. With my face still buried in his shoulder, I bit my lip to hold it all in.

"Ready to order?" he asked.

"Sure," I said, taking a step back and telling myself to relax.

As we stood in line, I studied the colorful chalkboard menu. Coffeehouses were plentiful in Boston, but none of them had quite the small-town ambience of Holly's. I had tried to order a latte the last time I was here. The server, looking around at her coworkers like she was about to give Rodney Dangerfield a run for his money, laughed and said, *If you want a latte, lady, go to Starbucks.* Which I totally would have, if there had *been* a Starbucks within a forty-mile radius. But things had apparently changed around here since then. An assortment of holiday lattes was now listed on the chalkboard, and a Wi-Fi password was taped to the front of the glass pastry display.

"Wi-Fi in Reindeer Falls," I said, shaking my head. "Who knew?"

Shane laughed. "I heard they're opening an Apple store next month. Right next to the feed store."

"Really?"

Shane gave me a sympathetic look. "All that money on a Harvard education, and for what? No, Caity. No Apple store."

I whacked him on the arm, grateful when the barista asked to take my order.

"Medium latte for me," I said. "And do you have anything with, like, marshmallow Peeps, and rainbow sprinkles, and maybe a dash of pumpkin spice for my friend here? Salt on the rim."

"Black coffee," said Shane, elbowing me out of the way. "Large." He'd been drinking black coffee since sophomore year of high school.

"You know," I said, "if you hadn't started chugging caffeine so young, maybe you wouldn't have stunted your brain development."

"Still so quick with the wit," he said, dumping what look liked six pennies into the tip cup.

"Still as generous as ever."

"I'm on a teacher's salary," he said, leaning against the counter as we waited for our coffees. "I'm not raking in the bucks like you, Miss Harvard Grad. So, tell me, what have you been up to? History professor? Assistant to Indiana Jones?"

"Unemployment."

"Oh," he said, eyebrows raised. "Let me guess...you were in the middle of singing *Happy Birthday, Mr. President* to your boss, when his wife walked in? He was forced to fire you to save his marriage?"

I rolled my eyes. "I didn't get fired."

"So, you're unemployed by choice?"

"What did I do, win the lottery? No, I was laid off. Ever hear of it?"

"Ah. I'm sorry. You want to talk about it?"

"I'm good."

We took our coffees back to the table in silence and sat down, facing each other properly for the first time in eight years. There were no students or parents around to interrupt this time. If we could manage to hold off on the back and forth insults for a few minutes, there might be an actual, adult conversation in the works. The thought was terrifying. Because eventually, one of us would have to bring it up. *It.* I'm not talking about the evil entity from the Stephen King novel, either. Believe me, I wish I were. That I could deal with.

"So," he said, taking a sip of coffee.

"So."

"If you don't want to talk about the fact that you were laid off because"—he paused for a moment, narrowing his eyes at me— "your job was outsourced to Minions?"

I laughed and shook my head.

"If you don't want to talk about *that*," he continued. "Then I've got another question for you..."

"No!" I said, slapping my hand on the table. "*No* questions."

"You don't even know what I was going to ask."

"Who do you think you're talking to? I found a whole notebook of those vile things under my bed this morning. What was *wrong* with us?" I took a rough swig of my latte.

Shane shrugged. "You've always had a dirty little mind under that quiet exterior. You know what they say."

"Yeah, yeah. But *you* were the one who brought it out of me." I tapped the side of my cup. "*You* were the bad influence."

"You loved me," said Shane.

Perhaps realizing what he'd just said, he started busying himself with unbuttoning and removing his coat. Underneath was a blue buffalo check flannel shirt. As he pushed up the sleeves, I caught the scent of his cologne. He couldn't still be wearing Abercrombie, could he? That was so high school. Like if I still shopped at Hollister and PacSun. Whatever it was, he smelled fantastic, and it took me straight back to the night before I'd left for college.

Shane had taken me out for ice cream. *Reparations for the past four years,* he'd laughed nervously over the phone. That phone call had come out of nowhere. We'd never done that type of thing before—going out, just the two of us. But it had been surprisingly easy. We'd stood in my front yard at the end of the night, the late August heat making that woodsy Abercrombie scent radiate from his skin, and I sensed that something was off. We were standing oddly far apart, even for us, and I'd waited, sort of holding my breath, while he stared into the distance at Dad's Buick Skyhawk parked in the driveway. Then he focused his eyes back on me, and they were so, so blue.

I think I'm in love with you, Caity. He'd said it slowly, almost as if he were realizing it himself for the first time. *I just wanted you to know, one time, before you left.* Then he'd taken a few hesitant steps toward me, holding out his hand. I stared at it for a few seconds, debating what I should do. Then I took his hand in mine and led him around to the side of the house—out of the possible view of my parents. I leaned against the siding, next to the kitchen air conditioner, which was peacefully whirring away, and I looked up into his eyes.

I didn't say those three words back. I knew I'd had a crush on him over the years. This was Shane Mitchell we were talking about—the adorable, over-the-top, drum-playing goofball. All of us band girls had crushes on Shane. But *love*? You didn't just go from the kind of relationship we had—playful insults and making each other laugh—to being in *love*. That wasn't how it worked. Where were the movies, and the flowers, and the dating anniversaries? Where were prom night, and Valentine's Day, and the angst-ridden promises to be together forever? We'd had none of that. True, we'd had a few fleeting moments over the years, but they had always been followed up by nothing. If Shane had wanted something, why had he gone and waited until time was up?

Even so, beside the gentle whir of the air conditioner, I pulled him toward me and kissed him. If he felt I was owed reparations for the way he'd treated me these past four years, then I was going to collect. Just to see. And I wasn't disappointed. The realization that this incredible thing that had come out of nowhere, was going to have to end just as quickly, put a sudden pit in my stomach. I knotted his T-shirt in my hands. *You idiot*, I'd finally whispered, pulling back, my hands still gripping the fabric. *Why now?* He only looked down at me and shook his head, both hands around my waist. I took a step to the side, ducking out of his grasp. *I have to go*, I'd said. *I'm leaving early in the morning. I'll...I'll call you.*

Plenty of phones at Harvard, but I never did.

"So." I cleared my throat. "Why'd you always want to play that dumb game with me, anyway? How come you never played it with any of your girlfriends?"

"I did," he said.

"Oh." I couldn't help but feel a bit let down. True, Questions was a dumb game, but it was *our* game. At least I'd thought it was.

"The problem was," he continued, "that they always answered them. No matter what I asked, they were always dying to let me in on their dirty little secrets."

"How difficult that must have been for you."

Shane laughed. "I never said it was difficult. What I'm saying is that those girls never left anything to the imagination. You and I both know there was only one girl who could keep me coming back." He gave me a wink.

That familiar, woodsy scent drifted once more across the table, and I realized I was starting to sweat. I took off my coat and tried to relax.

As we continued to chat, it seemed that neither of us was going to bring up the elephant in the room. I wasn't even sure if the elephant was the fact that Shane had told me he loved me, or the fact that after he told me, I'd disappeared from his life for eight years. We both had some explaining to do. I kept waiting for Shane to go first, but he never did. Instead, we spent the next hour tiptoeing gingerly around that night, reminiscing about anything and everything that had happened before that moment. Because that's all it really was, just a moment by the side of a house. A mere drop in the bucket.

I told him about how the three of us had come home to Reindeer Falls to perform our song together at the Christmas show. Being the high school music director, Shane had been involved with previous shows and was fairly close with Miss Annabeth. With a heavy sadness in his voice, he told me that he knew about her illness and about the community center possibly closing its doors.

"We donated some of the proceeds from the holiday concert to the community center," he said. "But it was just a drop in the bucket."

There we go again with the bucket analogy. I sighed. So many buckets. I picked up a spoon and began twirling it between my fingers.

"I wish I could think of a way to help," I said. "But I have no income right now, and I still have an apartment to pay for back in Boston."

My stomach clenched at the thought of my apartment and my rent. When I was in high school, going to Harvard seemed like a no-brainer. Even though I wasn't valedictorian, all my extracurricular musical activities made me the only student from Reindeer Falls High to be accepted. With a nearly full scholarship, it was a dream come true to be able to go. I was honored to attend such a prestigious school and to study history with some amazing professors. And, despite its nasty winters, I grew to love living in New England.

I stayed in Boston after graduation, using my history degree for a job at a textbook publishing house. Rent was sky-high and money was impossible to save. But until I'd lost my job, the thought of moving back home had never crossed my mind. I'd always told myself that I'd stayed in Boston because of the rich history and the abundance of jobs. But after just one day back at my parents' house, seeing the disorganization and the hoarding I had left behind, it was obvious that I'd simply run away.

I tried to lighten the mood after that, asking Shane about his teaching jobs and how his parents were doing—and it seemed to do the trick. My heart lifted at the brightness in his eyes as he talked about music, family, and all the things he loved the most.

CHAPTER 6

"*H*ow about you?" he asked, looking at me over the top of his cup. "Do you still play the piano at all?"

I shook my head. "I haven't touched a piano in years. Well, aside from Miss Annabeth's the other day, and you don't even want to know what song I chose to play."

Shane chuckled. "That's too bad. You were great."

"I just didn't have access to one back in Boston." I shrugged. "Not that I had the time, with school and everything. I tried to play Mom and Dad's piano last night, but it was buried and totally out of tune."

I'd returned home from the concert last night, happily aglow with nostalgia, and with the intention of sitting down at the piano and playing some holiday songs for my family. I was terribly saddened to find it buried beneath heaps of stuff. And after clearing out enough space to pull out the bench, I found that it was also horribly out of tune and unplayable. Instead of the old-fashioned family sing-along I'd been imagining, the four of us said our goodnights and traipsed rather gloomily off to bed.

"Buried?" A look of concern crossed Shane's face.

"Uh, yeah." I shifted uncomfortably. "Mom and Dad have always been a bit...disorganized."

"Nate's mentioned something about that a few times." Shane frowned. "He's a great kid. Sometimes he comes by my office just to chat."

"Really?" Shane and Nate sat around after school shooting the breeze? Was Shane handing out fatherly advice? Helping him with Algebra? He'd barely made it through high school himself. "What do you guys talk about?"

Shane shrugged. "Mostly school stuff or music. He says he likes to do his homework in my office because he can't concentrate at home. That's how the disorganization thing came up. Except he called your parents hoarders. I wasn't sure if he was just trying to be funny, you know? Everyone's watching those hoarding shows on TV."

"He wasn't exaggerating," I said, shaking my head, sad that Nate had confided this information to Shane instead of me. "I'm going over to talk to my parents about it this afternoon, actually. I want to give Nate his bedroom back for Christmas."

"You're a good sister. I know for a fact that Nate's missed you. This will mean a lot to him."

"I know," I mumbled, the truth of it stabbing me in the gut. "I'm going to try to make it up to him while I'm here."

"Which is until...when?"

"After Christmas?" I shrugged. "I think. I need to get back and start job hunting soon."

"*Stahht*," said Shane.

"Huh?"

"You said *staht* instead of start. You're a total Yankee now."

I laughed. "Am not."

"Am *naht*."

"Stop it!"

"*Stahp* it!"

"That's not even how a Boston accent works," I said, laughing. "There needs to be an 'r' in the word."

"Only a Yankee would know that."

"You know, with the Wi-Fi and the lattes, I was getting worried that Reindeer Falls might have changed too much. But nope. You're still an idiot." I wiped my brow in mock relief.

Our conversation, from that point on, was more comfortable and relaxed. Platonic. By the time we were ready to part ways, I was convinced that at some point over the past eight years—most likely the day after I'd left for college—Shane had realized that he wasn't in love with me at all. He'd probably met his new girlfriend and realized that any romantic feelings he thought he'd had for me were simply because everything had been changing too quickly after graduation. He'd confused love with nostalgia. It happens. I'd done it too.

We stood a few feet apart on the sidewalk in front of Holly's, with nosy townspeople strolling by, giving us curious looks. That was one thing I loved about the city—the anonymity of it. Back in Boston nobody looked at you twice. Here, I was probably big news. *Caitlin Cook's back from the big city, did you hear? Did you see her with that Shane Mitchell? How did* that *happen? Can that girl even talk? Always so quiet!*

"I could come by the house sometime and tune that piano for you," said Shane. "If you wanted me to. It would save you guys some money."

"Oh," I said. I hadn't been expecting that. "Like I said, the house is pretty messy. I don't know if you'll even be able to get the piano open."

"I could help with the cleanup, too," offered Shane. "I mean, if your parents agree to it. I'd like to help out Nate."

"That would be nice," I said, smiling. "Thank you."

"No problem. Let me give you my number."

I typed Shane's number into my phone and sent him a text. His phone vibrated in his hand and we were once again connected. We both stood there for a few seconds, unsure of how to proceed.

"So... I'll call you," I said, wincing as soon as the words came out of my mouth. So did Shane.

"Famous last words," he mumbled, squinting at me in the afternoon sun.

I took a few steps backward, my fight or flight response kicking in. I was never much of a fighter.

"I will," I said. "This time...I will. I promise." I waved my phone in the air for emphasis, and with an apologetic smile, beat a hasty retreat in the direction of my parents' shop.

I didn't look back as I raced up Main Street, nearly mowing over anybody in my path. That look on his face. Eight years later, and there was still no doubt that Shane had been hurt. Even if he'd eventually realized that he wasn't truly in love with me, it still must have hurt him that I'd never called. Never emailed. Never texted. We had been friends in our own strange way, and I'd simply abandoned him. When I had come home for that first Christmas break, with the intent of giving us a chance and attempting a long-distance relationship, I had found out that Shane was dating somebody he'd met at the University of Tennessee. With that kick to the gut, I laid low until it was time to fly back to Boston. I never saw him. He never knew about my change of heart. After that, I had one more good excuse to avoid coming home.

As he watched me speed-walk my way up the sidewalk, he probably figured it was the last time he'd see me for another eight years. I hated that that was the impression I had left. I never thought of myself as the type to run away, to abandon her loved ones and friends. But it was sinking in fast just how long I'd been doing that very thing. Not only had I abandoned Shane, but I'd left behind Mom, Dad, and Nate too. I'd made minimal effort to keep in touch with my closest friends and Miss Annabeth. I knew that I had made the right choice by going to Harvard—that wasn't the issue. The issue was that it had been four years since I'd graduated.

I smiled when I arrived at Christmas Past and saw the assortment of items that Mom and Dad had dragged out to the sidewalk. Two vintage baby buggies with huge wheels and elaborate canopies. Stacks of wooden suitcases with lots of interesting buckles and leather straps. A clothing rack filled with half-priced vintage clothing. I pulled down a high-necked, green velvet dress with a lace collar and cuffs and held it up, laughing at the thought of wearing it to the Christmas show. Michelle's reaction would be priceless. The price tag, however, wasn't so funny. Even at fifty percent off I couldn't afford it right now.

"You always were a conservative dresser, but this is getting ridiculous."

I jumped at the voice behind me, and turned around. "Shane! You scared me. I didn't realize you'd followed me."

"Sorry," he said. "It's just, the way you took off...I wanted to make sure you were okay. I mean, whatever happened all those years ago...it's in the past. No hard feelings, right?"

It's in the past. Finally, he'd said it. Finally, he'd confirmed that any feelings he'd once had for me were now gone.

"Of course," I said, shoving the dress back into the rack, but still hanging on to the sleeve. I needed something to fiddle with. "Like you said, it's in the past. We were young. And stupid." I forced a smile and tugged so hard on the sleeve that the whole dress fell off the hanger.

We stood there for what felt like an eternity, just staring down at the crumpled dress. I got the sense that we were each waiting for the other to elaborate on what exactly it *was* that had happened between us all those years ago. But what to say? I certainly wasn't going to attempt to go first, standing here in the street in broad daylight. Those types of conversations required alcohol and dim lighting. Instead, I crouched down, brushed a few leaves off the dress, and hung it back up.

"Good as new," I said, nodding awkwardly.

"So, um, is it okay if I go in to say hello to your parents?" asked Shane, changing the subject. "I haven't poked around Christmas Past in years. And, you know, I might be able to help talk to them about Nate."

"Of course," I said, relieved. "Come on."

The bells jingled as I pushed open the door and we stepped into the dim, cozy clutter of my parents' antique shop. On the wall behind the cashier's counter hung an enormous, terrifying painting of Ebenezer Scrooge screaming in fright as the Ghost of Christmas Past threw open his bed curtains. That painting had been in the store for as long as I could remember, and would alternate with Dad's collection of wide-eyed Victorian baby dolls for the job of giving me nightmares.

"Mom? Dad?" I shouted into the store. "Are you here?"

Shane followed me through several tightly packed racks of clothing. He nudged me in the back and raised his eyebrows as we passed a large, metal exam table with leather stirrups. I snorted.

"I don't even want to know," I said.

"Your parents are so interesting."

"If you think that's interesting, there are a bunch of boxes at the house marked *Doll Heads*."

Shane whistled.

"We're in the back, love!" shouted Mom.

We followed the sound of sandpapering into the back room of the store. Dad was down on his knees sanding a table. Mom was leaning against the workbench, wearing an oversized "Harvard Mom" sweatshirt, her frizzy reddish waves pulled back into a ponytail.

"Mr. Mitchell!" she said, putting her coffee mug down and shaking his hand. "I didn't know Caity had brought a friend!" She shot me a meaningful look.

"Hello, Mrs. Cook," said Shane.

"Please, call me Sandy!"

"Only if you'll call me Shane. That 'Mr. Mitchell' stuff is for my students."

"Of course, *Shane*," said Mom, beaming. I rolled my eyes, but she ignored me. "The concert last night was wonderful, by the way. It's just what we needed to kick off the holidays!"

"Thank you," said Shane. "The kids worked hard. Especially Nate. He nailed his trumpet solo."

"We're grateful that he's taken so well to music," said Dad, standing up and brushing off his knees. "Kids these days. You never know." He bobbed his head up and down, his mustache twitching nervously. Then he hurried back to sanding the table.

"Nate's a great kid," said Shane, glancing at me. "That's sort of why I stopped in with Caitlin."

"Can we talk for a few minutes?" I asked.

"Of course, love," said Mom. "Brian, get back over here. Would you two like some coffee?"

"No, thanks. We just had some at Holly's."

Mom gave me another one of her meaningful looks. I really wished she'd stop doing that.

"Anyway," I said. "I had a look in Nate's bedroom this morning, and I noticed that half of what's in there doesn't actually belong to him."

A look of guilt crossed Mom's face. "There's been a bit of spillover, I won't deny it."

"It's more than a bit, Mom. And it's kind of a problem. Nate needs his own space. He's been doing his homework in Shane's office because it's too cramped for him at home. Did you know that? And when's the last time he had a friend over?"

"Oh, I don't know." Mom gazed thoughtfully up at the ceiling. "Brian, do you remember the last time Nate had a friend over?"

"A friend?" Dad's mustache twitched again as he mulled it over. "Sure, sure. I remember. I forget his name. Brown hair. Body like a stick bug. Jumpy fella."

I held back a laugh at the thought of Dad calling somebody else jumpy.

"Bradley?" asked Mom.

"Bradley. That's it. They were playing with those phones at the kitchen counter. Both of them, sitting right next to each other staring at those screens. I walked into the room, kid jumped a mile high. Kids today." Dad shook his head.

"But the last time Bradley came over was before Halloween!" said Mom.

"*See?*" I said. "While I'm back in Reindeer Falls, I really want to help you and Dad get organized. At the very least, I want to give Nate his own space back. But I'd also like for us to be able to fit a Christmas tree in the living room. Be honest, Mom. You weren't planning on getting a tree this year, were you?"

Mom sighed and closed her eyes. "There are just so many boxes of doll heads."

"Factory closed last year in Gatlinburg," added Dad. "First come, first served. Your mother and I, we filled the truck."

"You have plans for those doll heads, Dad?" I wasn't even being sarcastic. Shane was spot-on when he said that my parents were interesting. Mom and Dad saw potential in everything. For all I knew, refurbished doll heads were going for fifty bucks a pop.

He shrugged. "Never know what you'll need someday. Best to take it now, worry about details later."

Or maybe not.

"Will you at least let me try to help you get more organized?" I asked. "I'm not expecting the house to look like something out of a magazine. I know that's not realistic. I just want to try to make it *better*. For Nate."

"He'll be applying to colleges soon," added Shane. "You want him to have a good home environment so he can keep up his grades. And you also want him to have a home that he's going to look forward to coming back to."

46

Mom and Dad looked at each other, their eyes speaking volumes, and I knew that was all it was going to take. A lump formed in my throat.

"We'd love your help, Caity," said Mom, softly. "We don't want to do anything that might drive Nate away."

"I know," I said, reaching over to squeeze her hand. "There's one other thing I want to do before we get to Nate's room, though. I want to clear the area around the piano and make it playable again. Shane's even offered to tune it for us."

"That would be wonderful," said Mom, beaming at him. "Thank you so much. Now tell me, will your parents be coming back from their retirement community for Christmas?"

Shane nodded. "They'll be staying with me. Owning the house is bizarre. It's like we've swapped roles, and now they're the ones coming home from college. I feel like I should lay down some rules when they get here."

"No girls over after ten o'clock? That sort of thing?" asked Dad, snorting loudly. Mom elbowed him in the ribs.

"Exactly," said Shane, giving my father a wink.

"Where'd you go to school, again?" asked Mom. "No one ever needs to ask where Caity went!" She laughed as she motioned to her Harvard sweatshirt. She must have a hundred of those things. Dad and Nate, too. Out of guilt for not coming home very often to visit, I tended to send a lot of gifts. They knew me by name at the Harvard Coop.

"University of Tennessee," said Shane. "It wasn't my first choice, but it worked out."

From the brief glance that he gave me, I knew exactly what he was thinking about. That one afternoon in the band room. I'd never forgotten it either.

CHAPTER 7

*T*t was February of senior year, and I had stopped by the music department after school to pick up my flute. Normally, at that time of day, there would have been band kids lining the hallways and hanging out in the rehearsal room. Our teachers had always encouraged the music department as a safe and welcoming place to spend time with friends after school. It was sort of an extension of the community center.

On that particular day, however, the hallways were deserted. It was the Friday before a long weekend, and hanging around school after the final bell was a hard sell even for band kids. I opened the door to the rehearsal room and headed for the locked instrument cabinets. I'd taken out my flute, and was just about to shut the cabinet, when a crinkling sound alerted me to the fact that I wasn't alone. Sitting on the floor at the back of the room—partially hidden amongst the percussion instruments—was Shane. He had his forearms resting on his knees, a wrinkled piece of paper in his hands.

"Bad news from the clinic?" I'd joked, slamming the cabinet shut and re-locking it. His head jerked up, as if he hadn't even heard me come in.

"Huh?"

"Never mind." I started heading for the exit, but paused halfway. "You okay?" I was expecting him to say he'd flunked another English test. He tended to do that. He'd occasionally get lazy, fail a test, and then blow the teacher out of the water a few weeks later with a doctoral level essay on Huck Finn, or whatever. The way he could just turn his intellect on and off like that drove me crazy. The way he *chose* to turn it on and off like that drove me crazier. Still, I'd never seen him looking quite so blue before. Certainly not over a test.

He looked up and waved the paper in the air. "I didn't get in."

Oh. I should have known.

Senior year was full of mailman-induced anxiety. The sight of Pete Cooper barreling down our road in his little white truck, taking out wildlife without remorse, and screeching to a halt in front of our mailbox, had given my stomach a flip or two of its own. But I'd received my Harvard acceptance letter back in November, and was already starting to forget that others were still waiting for their fat or skinny envelopes to arrive. The one-page letter Shane was holding should have tipped me off. I walked up the risers to the back of the room and sat down on the floor next to him. It was kind of cozy back there, barricaded behind a row of drums.

"May I?" I asked, placing my fingers around the letter. He let it go without any resistance. The letterhead was from the Berklee College of Music in Boston. *We regret to inform you...*

Shane had auditioned on piano back in December. While he was strictly a percussionist at school, piano was his real passion. He'd told me once, on the bus, that his grandmother had taught him how to play when he was eight. Sometimes I would watch him during class, his fingers silently tapping out songs on his desk. I'd only heard him play for real a few times. Once when he thought he was alone in the band room after school, and once at Heavenly Peace. My grandmother had been living there at the time, and I'd gone for a visit a few weeks before Christmas. Shane was there, playing the piano in the dining room for a small audience. He'd had his back to the door and didn't see me.

At school, he never fought me for the job of piano accompanist with the choir or the jazz band, and I wondered if maybe he'd regretted that. Maybe the extra practice and the additional extracurricular activities would have helped him to get in. I doubted it. Extra practice or not, he was a better piano player than I ever dreamed of being.

"I'm sorry," I said. "It wasn't the audition though, was it?"

Shane leaned his head back against the wall. "Probably not."

"GPA will get you like that."

"SATs too."

"Right." I didn't ask what his scores were. Then I thought of something. "How'd you get this letter, anyway? You spend enough time in the principal's office to get your mail there?"

Shane laughed softly and shook his head. "I went home after school. I was there about five minutes before I heard Pete coming. I think he may have hit a turtle."

"So many casualties." I sighed.

"I went out to the mailbox and there it was."

"Crushed turtle?"

"The *letter*, smarty. My parents weren't home from work yet, and I didn't want to be there when they did get home, so I ran back here."

"Like Forrest Gump?"

He pinched the bridge of his nose between his fingers and sighed. "I didn't *actually* run, Caity."

I bit my lip and waited a few moments before speaking again.

"Why are you afraid to tell your parents?" I asked. "They seem nice. Well, your mom seems nice. Your dad..." I shuddered.

Shane's father was the county medical examiner. He didn't look like what you would expect, which I think made it worse. He looked a lot like Shane. Blue eyes, big smile. The fact that someone so jovial could spend their workdays carving up dead bodies gave me the creeps. Shane's mother had been his assistant back before they were married. Family legend has it that she handed him a scalpel one fine afternoon, watched him slice into some poor schlub's abdomen, and then he asked her out for drinks. The rest is history. I didn't know how Shane slept at night.

"You got a problem with my dad?" he asked, turning to look at me.

"Of *course,* I have a problem with your dad," I said. "His career is horrifying. That's not my point. My point is that your parents are medical professionals. They're going to be disappointed in you for choosing a career in music no matter where you go to college."

Shane laughed. "You always know how to cheer me up, Cook."

"What'd you want to go to Berklee for, anyway?" I continued, encouraged by the sound of his laughter. "You think the 'One time at band camp' stories are bad now? You go to Berklee, and it's nothing but band camp stories. Twenty-four seven. It would literally drive you insane. And the worst part? The last thing you ever heard, before you went bonkers, would be a story about what some idiot did with his trombone. Is that really what you want, Shane? Is it?"

He was watching me now—eyebrows raised, eyes filled with amusement—as if I were a block of cheese that had just started speaking. I suppose that probably was the most words I'd ever spoken to him all at once.

"What's so great about Boston, anyway?" I continued, still on a roll. Still enjoying the curious feeling of ease I suddenly had, sitting there with Shane. "There are plenty of amazing music schools right here in Tennessee."

Sure, I was heading to Boston, but that was to go to Harvard. Shane lived a few hours away from Nashville. It really didn't make a lot of sense.

Shane shrugged and nudged my foot with his. "Maybe I wanted to see the look on your face when I walked into the Harvard Coop and ordered myself a beer."

"You're not old enough to drink."

"I'd get a fake ID."

I put my head in my hands and mumbled, "The Coop's a bookstore."

"So, I'd have ordered myself a book." I felt his shoulder shrug against mine. "If I happened to get a world-class music education along the way, all the better."

I laughed. "You don't need to go all the way to Boston to keep bugging me, Shane. I'll be back to visit. We'll stay in touch. You can follow me on Twitter if you'd like."

"Those posts should be thrilling. Hashtag reading books. Hashtag Friday nights alone in my dorm."

"I wouldn't be making jokes about academics right now, if I were you." I swatted the side of his knee with my hand. Shane playfully swatted me back, and before I realized what was happening, he'd scooped my hand right up into his. We both sat there staring at our unmoving hands for a good ten seconds, my heart beating rapidly. Any feeling of ease I'd had, totally gone

"You ever wish you could go back in time?" he asked, quietly, his thumb suddenly stroking the side of my hand. "And, you know, change some stuff?"

I swallowed hard, caught between being unable to move and wanting to do some things I'd only ever dreamed about.

"Um, sometimes, yeah," I said. "You just have to be really careful with time travel, you know? You change one little thing and suddenly Reindeer Falls is post-apocalyptic." I laughed nervously.

"That escalated quickly," said Shane. "No, I'd be pretty careful about what I changed. Nothing earth-shattering."

"Like what, then?"

I shifted on the cold, hard floor so I could look at his face. I knew exactly how I would answer the question, if I had no filter and no shame. I'd tell him that I would go back in time and work my hardest to change my personality from shy and introverted, to chatty and flirty and fun. Life was so much easier for girls like that. The sort of girls he'd taken to all the dances and proms, and paid all his attention to—except for when he was bored on the bus, or depressed at the back of the band room.

"I think I'd just try to figure out sooner which things in life are really important. Before it was too late." He met my eyes and my breath caught in my throat. Then he picked his rejection letter up off the floor with his free hand and dangled it in the air.

Right. Things that were really important in life, like getting into the college of your choice. I gently pulled my hand out of his grasp, and he rolled himself onto his knees so that he was facing me. Then he reached out and pulled a section of hair away from my head, running his fingers all the way down to the tips. When he got to the bottom, he playfully coiled it around his fingers before letting it fall back onto my shoulder. I thought for sure that he was about to kiss me. If I had been that forward, flirty, fun version of Caitlin Cook, I'd have leaned in and done it myself. Instead, we just blinked at each other until finally, in one of the greatest disappointments of my life, he stood up.

"Thanks for the talk," he said. "I think I'm ready to go home now, and uh...face the music." He made a dorky face and raked his hand through his hair.

"No problem." I didn't stand up. Wasn't sure if I could. Shane smiled down at me, looking as if he were about to say something else. Instead, he nodded briskly, then turned and headed for the door. I lost sight of him, since I was sitting behind a bass drum, but there was a pause before I heard the twist of the door handle.

"I'm going to hold you to that visit," he called back. "I'm going to miss our little chats."

"We can ride the Greyhound bus back and forth to Nashville and play Questions," I said, glad that he couldn't see me. My heart was beating like the bass drum I was hiding behind, and my cheeks were burning up.

There was another pause, followed by a nervous jiggling of the door handle.

"I'll see you Tuesday, Cook."

The door swung shut.

When Tuesday came, it was business as usual between us. And as it turned out, I never did come back to visit. Not with Shane, at least.

CHAPTER 8

$\mathcal{I}$t was Saturday morning, and I was tired.

I'd tossed and turned for hours last night, a surreal version of my entire life swirling around in my mind. Harvard. Shane. Alex Trebek. I was on Jeopardy and I'd screamed at poor Alex, "But Questions was *our* game!" I'd woken briefly with a jolt, and then I was off again, having a beer with Shane at the Harvard Coop, which was also a bowling alley, which was also an antique shop. Doll heads lined the racks of rental shoes. I rested my head on Shane's shoulder as we sat side-by-side at the bar. *I'm glad you're here,* I'd said. And then, without warning, or an ounce of decorum, I was off my barstool and sitting on his lap. While it was a completely mortifying thing to consider doing in real life, it hadn't felt the slightest bit wrong within my dream. Things were just starting to get good when my alarm went off. With a disgruntled moan, the dream faded away, and a strange sort of heaviness settled into my chest.

It was nine thirty now, and the heaviness in my chest was quickly being replaced by nervous anticipation. Shane was coming over at ten o'clock to tune the piano. Mom and Dad were at the shop until later, and Nate was still upstairs asleep until who knew when. Shane and I would be practically alone, the thought of which terrified me. I switched on the TV in the living room for background noise, settling on QVC. It was only nine thirty in the morning, but there was David, test-driving a plate of baby back ribs and licking the sauce off his fingers. For only one hundred dollars I could get five pounds of those bad boys auto-delivered every ninety days. The butterflies in my stomach calmed down a bit. David had moved on to an indoor grill that would take up all of my counter space, but was guaranteed to change the way I thought about meat, when the doorbell rang.

I grabbed a bottle of furniture polish and a rag, so it wouldn't look like I'd just been sitting around watching QVC all morning, and opened the door. Shane was holding a laptop case in one hand and a cardboard coffee tray in the other.

"What'd you ring the doorbell with?" I asked. He raised one eyebrow at me in response. I laughed and took the coffees. "You didn't have to bring these. Let me give you some money."

Shane waved me off. "It's no big deal."

"Thanks," I said, taking a grateful sip. I'd tried to make coffee when I woke up this morning, but the box of K-Cups Mom kept in the microwave was empty. The old-fashioned coffeemaker was residing with my computer monitor on the front porch, so I'd been suffering caffeine free all morning. "Come on in."

Shane took a few steps into the house and looked around. I felt like he was one of the psychologists on those hoarding shows, trying not to look too shocked and horrified by what he was seeing, while simultaneously evaluating if there was enough time left on Earth to even make a dent.

"So, um, the piano's this way," I said, motioning for him to follow. "Watch your step." I guided him through the path I had begun carving between piles of things, until we got to the living room.

Without a word about the mess, Shane dragged the coffee table closer to the piano and set up his laptop. From the inside pocket of his coat, he produced a small piano tuning hammer. Then he sat down on the piano bench and cracked his knuckles.

"You're pretty high-tech," I said, looking at the laptop. Some sort of piano tuning software was on the screen.

"Gotta be," said Shane. "Piano tuning's a cutthroat world."

"Do you have turf wars with Norm?" I asked. Norm had been the local piano tuner when I was a kid.

"Nope. Norm died. I'm the only game in town now."

Shane played a few melancholy chords while I mulled over the fact that Norm was no longer with us. Then he broke into the lively strains of "The Entertainer." It sounded horribly out of tune and amazing all at the same time, and it chased all thoughts of poor Norm straight out of my head. I couldn't help but smile as I watched his fingers flying around the keys. The Berklee admissions staff were fools. Shane could play by ear, an ability I'd always dreamed of having. Instead, I was a slave to the sheet music.

Shane stopped abruptly and whistled. "This'll take me at least an hour. You might need to mute that." He jerked his head toward the TV. "So the microphone can hear the notes."

"Oh, right." I pushed the mute button on the remote, and we were instantly swallowed up by the silence. "Should I leave you to it? I can go in another room."

Shane shrugged. "I don't mind the company."

"Okay."

I sat down on the couch and watched David silently wood-chipping his way through an ear of corn, while Shane opened up the top of the piano and set to work. He tested and adjusted each key, starting from the low notes and working his way up. I couldn't possibly just sit there watching muted QVC for the next hour. I mean, I *could*. It certainly wouldn't have been the first time. But with Shane working so hard on our piano, I felt like I should be doing something too. I walked into the kitchen, grabbed a trash bag, and came back into the living room. I knew it was the plan to get Nate's room cleaned up first, but I couldn't exactly barge in there while the kid was still asleep. I may as well start clearing out a space for the Christmas tree.

Shane and I worked in companionable silence for the next hour—me, trying not to dispose of anything Mom and Dad might miss, and Shane, efficiently working his way up the keyboard. We made occasional small talk, but were mainly focused on our tasks. I was doing more stacking and rearranging than throwing away, but by the time Shane had reached the high notes, I'd cleared a Christmas-tree-sized area in front of the living room window.

I stepped back to admire my work just as Shane was closing up the top of the piano. He sat back down on the bench to test out his work. I was expecting a bit of Mozart, or maybe some more ragtime. Instead, he started to play the left-hand accompaniment of "Heart and Soul"—the simple duet that you learn as a child. He smiled at me over his shoulder. Like a magnet, I sat down on the bench beside him, plinking out the melody with my right hand. We played it through a couple of times, and then Shane gently nudged me down the bench with his elbow so he could play a fancy little number all across the keyboard. I rolled my eyes. He slid back over, and I started plinking out the melody again. He reached behind me and played a little flourish on the high notes. I jabbed him with my elbow.

"Stop showing off," I muttered, and he smiled. "Get up for a sec."

We stopped playing and stood up so I could lift the seat of the piano bench. I took out a book of sheet music and flipped through until I got to "I'll Be Home for Christmas," the song we would be performing in a few short weeks at the Christmas show. I sat back down and took a deep breath. Shane stood behind me.

"Here goes nothing."

I started off a bit rusty, playing much too slowly and stumbling over many of the notes. But as I went along, it all started coming back much faster than I had expected. It was like riding a bicycle. Sure, you swiveled your front wheel manically back and forth a few times, slammed into a couple of telephone poles and parked cars, but eventually you figured it out. Knowing that Shane was watching and listening right behind me had me on edge. My hands were shaking. But still, the act of making music —after having bottled it up for the past eight years, focusing only on school and work—was pure joy, mistakes and all. Right on cue, Shane turned the pages for me, and when I reached the repeat sign at the end, I went back to the beginning and played it through again. When I neared the ending the second time, Shane sat down beside me on the bench and waited for me to finish.

"So... how did it feel?" he asked, as I held the final note.

My dirty, dirty mind—the one I thought I had left back in high school, between the pages of a black and white chevron notebook—went ahead and took those words to a whole other level. My stomach fluttered and my foot slipped abruptly off the sustain pedal. The room went quiet.

"Really good," I said, in a husky voice. I cleared my throat. "I mean, I'm not sure how it *sounded*. But...it felt good. I never even realized I had missed it so much."

I patted the top of the piano like a dog, suddenly doing awkward things because every inch of my body was acutely aware of how close we were sitting. His right leg was pressed up against mine, and his right elbow brushed against my left as he tapped his index finger lightly against Middle C. He was nervous around me. I could feel it.

"Well, it sounded great," he said. "And you were much more confident the second time through. Give it a few more weeks and you'll be as good as ever."

"Thanks," I said, turning my head slightly to the left to sneak a look at him. As soon as I did, I remembered my dream. In the blink of an eye I could be sitting on Shane's lap. My little brother could walk in at any moment to find his sister home from the big city, mauling his music teacher. A giggle escaped me.

"What's so funny?"

"Nothing," I said, trying to quickly think up a lie, because if I knew Shane, he wasn't going to let this go.

"You were thinking of something dirty, weren't you?"

"What? No!" My face flushed. "I just thought of a joke I heard."

"A dirty one?"

"No. Geez. What's with you? Just a regular joke."

"Let's hear it."

"I don't even remember it." I shrugged and played a few random chords. "Something about a rabbi, a priest, and a rowboat. Very offensive. It's best if I don't repeat it."

"That's very mature of you," said Shane. "How about if you tell me your joke, I'll tell you a secret?" He looked down at the keyboard and starting playing a slow, swingy little melody.

"I don't think I want to know any of your secrets," I said, crinkling my nose. "Especially if it's about how many Kathy Ireland Swimsuit Editions you have under your bed."

Shane laughed. "Wow, that was an elaborate stab. Harvard was well worth the money. But, no. That's not it. It's about the night I told you I was in love with you." He said it very casually, as if stating a fact from a history book, before loudly laying on those three classic suspense notes. *Dun-Dun-Duuuun!*

It was suddenly quite hard to breathe. I knew we were going to talk about it eventually, but I hadn't expected him to just bring it up out of the blue. But there it was—three suspenseful notes, loaded with meaning and hanging in the air like a Friday afternoon *Days of Our Lives* cliffhanger. The fact that he could bring it up in such a casual manner confirmed what I already knew.

"You didn't mean it," I said, attempting to beat him to the punch. "That's no big secret, Shane. It's in the past, like you said. You probably woke up Nate, by the way."

He took his hands off the keyboard and swung around sideways to face me, his brow furrowed. "Of course, I *meant* it."

"How could you have meant it?" I asked, standing and walking toward the window, needing to put some distance between us. "We barely even knew each other in high school."

"Seriously?" he said. "All those bus rides? Our talks? Believe it or not...I meant it."

"Oh."

That was all I could think to say. *Oh.* Everything I had talked myself into believing since that first heartbreaking visit home from college was beginning to come undone. He'd actually meant it. And if he'd meant it back then, did that mean that he still had feelings for me?

"If you meant it so much," I said, quietly, "why'd you go and wait until the night before I left to tell me?"

"Dunno," he said, looking away and running his hand down the piano keys. "Because I was seventeen?"

I sighed. I couldn't argue with that. I'd seen our baby-faced pictures in the high school lobby. That strange ache returned to my chest. "So, what's your big secret, then?"

"The rule was that you had to tell me your joke first."

I rolled my eyes and told him a lame joke I'd heard from my dad.

Satisfied, he swung back around to face the piano. "My secret is that after I left you that night, I stole a bottle of vodka out of my dad's liquor cabinet and drank screwdrivers until I passed out. That was the first and last time I ever did anything like that. You were the only girl to ever drive me to drink." He chuckled as he played a few chords with his left hand.

I was about to point out that if he'd been driven to drink, it had been through nobody's fault but his own—that it wasn't *me* who had chosen to make an angst-ridden declaration of love at the most inconvenient time ever, but *him*—when he stopped playing and looked up at *Dogs Playing Poker*, the painting which had hung above our piano since the dawn of time.

"You ever wish you could go back in time?" he asked, still looking at the dogs. Then he looked down and played a few bluesy chords in a way that was almost comical, but I didn't laugh.

What I wanted to do was sit down beside him and say yes. I wanted to tell him that if I could go back in time, I would have called him the moment I'd arrived in Boston. I wanted to tell him that the reason I hadn't called was because it had taken everything I had just to keep up with my classes, and if I'd thrown a brand-new long-distance relationship into the mix, I would have completely buckled. Something would have had to give, and I hadn't wanted it to be us. I wanted to tell him that I had come back for him that first Christmas, but it had been too late. I wanted him to know that it had all just been a series of immaturity and bad timing, and that if I could do it all over again, I'd make sure that *this* time we had our chance.

But then Nate walked in, blurry-eyed and in his boxer shorts, and the opportunity was gone.

CHAPTER 9

"*S*o, in general, how many butter churns do you actually need?"

Mom, Dad, and I were standing shoulder-to-shoulder, peering into Nate's tiny closet. Shane had gone home hours earlier, right after Nate had walked into the room in his underwear. Between that, and the awkward turn our conversation had taken, it was clearly time for him to leave. We promised that we would catch up with each other again in a few days, and I'd watched him walk back to his car with a heaviness in my chest. I'd kept my phone in my back pocket, just in case he decided to text, but all was silent. Mom and Dad came home from the shop in the early afternoon, and the Cook Family Christmas Cleanup had officially begun.

Sort of.

"It's not about what we need, Caity," said Mom. "It's about demand. Antique butter churns are highly collectible. They fly off the shelves!"

"If they fly off the shelves, why are there so many of them in this closet?"

"Overstock," said Dad. "Extra."

"How can you have extra of something that's flying off the shelves?"

Neither Mom nor Dad seemed able to work out the logic, so I moved along.

"Look, new rule," I said. "Nate's closet isn't for overstock. Nate's closet is for Nate's stuff. However odd it may be." I motioned to what looked like a Chewbacca costume dangling from a hanger. "Agreed?"

Mom and Dad looked nervously at each other, communicating through a series of shrugs and nods, clicks and whistles. Finally, they turned to me.

"Agreed," they said in unison.

"Great."

I glanced at Nate, who was sprawled across his bed with one arm flung over his eyes. He didn't move his arm, but he did smile.

We spent the next few hours moving butter churns and cardboard boxes into the attic, which was, surprisingly, the one place yet to be cluttered. Every so often Dad would peek inside a box and pull out something interesting to show us. A View-Master reel of the Smoky Mountains. A postcard from the 1939 New York World's Fair. A photograph of Leona Bainbridge, the first woman to go over Reindeer Falls in a barrel.

"She was the first *person* to go over Reindeer Falls in a barrel," said Nate. "Never mind the fact that she was a woman."

"The *only* person to go over Reindeer Falls in a barrel," pointed out Mom.

"You have her death certificate in there too?" I asked, peering into the box and making Dad snort.

Eventually, everything that was left in Nate's room belonged to Nate, and the four of us stood in the bedroom doorway admiring our work.

Sort of.

"It looks too bare," said Nate. He had a point. With all the boxes and butter churns removed, his TV was now sitting on the floor surrounded by dust bunnies, rubber bands, and paper clips. It looked worse than my dorm room on move-out day. I looked at my phone.

"Hey, it's only four o'clock," I said. "How about we go out to dinner and then make a trip to Walmart? We can get Nate a TV stand, and some Christmas decorations, and maybe on the way home we could pick out a tree?" I bounced up and down on my toes.

Mom and Dad had been a bit rattled when they'd first come home and seen the space I'd cleared away for a Christmas tree, while Shane had been tuning the piano. But once I'd reassured them that their boxes of doll heads, old-timey kazoos and yellowed, vintage christening gowns were still there, only rearranged, they seemed genuinely happy with the progress I'd made. They no longer had any excuse not to go out and get a tree.

"I don't think we can all fit in the Harvester," said Dad.

"You're in luck," said Nate. "I'm heading over to Brad's. You guys can go without me."

"You'll do no such thing!" I said. "It's been too long since the four of us have done anything together."

"Weren't we just doing something together for the past two hours?"

"That's different. Besides, I'm trying to pick out stuff for *your* room, you ingrate."

Nate rolled his eyes, but made no further argument.

"But how will we fit?" asked Mom.

"We'll take two cars," I explained. Apparently, one needed a Harvard degree to work out the solution to transporting four people and a Christmas tree. "You and Nate take your car, and I'll go with Dad in the Harvester." I'd been sort of dying for a ride in that thing ever since I laid eyes on it. I mean, it was Mater, for Pete's sake.

And so, for the first time in a long while, the entire Cook family headed out for a night on the town. Sure, we were in separate cars, and a night on the town in Reindeer Falls meant pizza and a Walmart run. But as I climbed into the Harvester next to Dad, watching his mustache twitch and bob the entire way to Pizza Hut because the smile never left his face, I knew that *where* we were going was totally beside the point.

* * *

CLEMSON'S CHRISTMAS Tree Farm was a happening place on a Saturday night. A boombox, blasting holiday tunes, had been placed outside on a wooden chair, with about a mile of extension cords running across the grass and into a small shed. On a stool outside the shed sat Rudy Clemson, wearing a pair of flashing reindeer antlers and sipping from a paper cup. A king upon his throne.

"Hellooooo, Cooks!" he shouted, as soon as we'd walked through the gates. "I wasn't sure if we'd be seeing you here this year!"

"Of course, you were going to see us! Don't be silly! We *always* get a tree." Mom glanced nervously at me as she dragged us over to say hello. "You remember Caitlin, don't you? She's been living in Boston for a while now—she went to Harvard, you know? — but she's come home this year for Christmas!" Mom threw her arm around my shoulders and gave me a squeeze.

"Of course, I remember the lovely Caitlin," said Rudy, hoisting his paper cup into the air. "'Tis the season!"

"'Tis the season!" I replied, hoisting my empty hand into the air. "It's nice to see you again, Rudy."

"Hold on, hold on," he said, turning toward the shed. "No empty hands at Clemson's Christmas Tree Farm! Margaret! Bring the Cooks out some hot cocoa!"

Like magic, Margaret Clemson appeared in the doorway. She was draped in an enormous, hand-knit red poncho, and was already holding a tray full of steaming paper cups.

"How are you, dears?" she asked, offering each of us a cup. When the Clemsons weren't farming Christmas trees, they were avid antique collectors, and had grown close with my family over the years. "And Caitlin. You must be home because of poor Annabeth? She finally broke down and told us everything at knitting club last week. What do you think of my poncho?" She spun around to give us a better look.

"It's beautiful," I said.

"And so stylish!" said Mom, reaching out and squeezing a pom-pom.

"I delivered a tree to Annabeth just this morning," chimed in Rudy, giving his wife's poncho some serious side-eye. "That music teacher came by and ordered one for her yesterday. Sheldon something. Or was it Sherlock?"

"Shane?" I asked, surprised.

"That's the fella!"

My hands were already warm from my cup of hot chocolate, but suddenly my heart was feeling quite melty, too. Shane hadn't mentioned anything about buying Miss Annabeth a tree when he'd been at our house this morning. I noticed Mom staring at me and quickly went back to admiring Margaret's poncho.

"Your friend Emma's back in town, too," said Margaret. "For about a week now. She's renting out the room over our barn!" She let out a loud laugh and elbowed her husband.

"Emma's living above your barn?" I choked on my hot chocolate. Last I'd heard, Emma had been living in New York and modeling for places like Gap and H&M. Why she'd be renting a room above a barn was beyond me. I really did stink at keeping in touch with my friends.

"Her parents moved to Arizona several years ago, so she doesn't have family to stay with," said Margaret, heaving herself onto the stool next to Rudy. "I told her she could probably get a real nice room over at the Poinsettia Cottage, but she insisted on the barn!"

Before I could question Margaret further, a young family came over to pay for their Christmas tree. We thanked the Clemsons for the hot chocolate, and wandered off to pick out a tree of our own.

Thirty minutes later, the Cook Family Christmas Tree was secured in the back of the Harvester, and Dad and I were bouncing along the winding back roads toward home. I couldn't wait to get back to the house and start decorating, but the back roads just kept winding on and on. After living in the city for so long, I'd forgotten just how rural it was out here. I double-checked that my cell phone was in my purse and fully charged, just in case. It was in there, and so was a text from Shane. Like a teenager, I angled the phone so that Dad couldn't see, and opened the message. My stomach fluttered as I imagined a million things Shane might have said. Only half of them G-rated.

Nate's not traumatized, is he?

Or he was asking about my brother.

He's repressing the memory as we speak, I replied.

The best possible outcome.

I smiled and stared at the screen, my thumbs hovering over the keyboard. I had the urge to reply with something flirty, but I had no idea where to begin, or if it was even appropriate. Sure, Shane had admitted that he had truly been in love with me back in high school. But still, eight years had gone by. I didn't even know if he had a girlfriend.

That was sweet, getting a tree for Miss Annabeth, I typed. Then I held my breath as I watched his little typing bubbles disappear and reappear a few times.

"Good pizza," said Dad.

"Huh?" I jumped.

"The pizza," said Dad. "Good."

"Oh, right." I switched off my phone and threw it back into my purse. "Very good pizza. Cheese inside the crust. Who knew?"

"They have Pizza Huts in Boston, don't they?" asked Dad, giving me a concerned glance.

"Of course," I said. "But I haven't eaten at one in ages. There are so many better restaurants around."

"Not that place you brought us last time we visited?" asked Dad.

I laughed. The last time my family was in Boston, I'd taken them to an upscale pizza joint in Harvard Square where Dad somehow ended up with a white, sauce-less pizza, topped with nothing but sliced garlic and lumps of ricotta.

"I *like* that place," I said. "If you know what to order, it's actually very good."

Dad shook his head. "I'll leave the fancy pizzas to you, Caity. Just give me a deep-dish Meat Lover's and I'm a happy man." He nodded his head. "Meat."

As we emerged at last into civilization—aka downtown Reindeer Falls, Population: Nobody after seven p.m.—I noticed signs had been stuck into the ground advertising the Christmas show at the community center. As if there were anybody in town who didn't already know about it.

"Do you want to swing by Shane Mitchell's house?" asked Dad.

"What?" I jumped again. "Why?"

"To see the lights."

"What lights?"

"You haven't heard? Shane's been doing a big display ever since he bought his parents' house. I'll show you. Call Mom."

"Okay." I made the call and told my mother where we were headed. Then Dad made a right turn at the lights, rather than the left that would have taken us home.

CHAPTER 10

$\mathcal{I}$'d been to Shane's house once in my life. It was junior year, and his parents were out of town for the week at a medical examiner's convention. Word had quickly spread amongst the band kids that there'd be a party at the Mitchell house on Saturday night. Shane and his parents lived in a grand, old Colonial, with a hot tub on the back porch, and an inground swimming pool that lit up purple and blue at night.

It being a band party, Mom and Dad had no qualms about me going. Typical band parties involved a bunch of kids sitting around in somebody's basement, eating pizza and watching Seth Rogen movies. The parents of the host always sat upstairs at the kitchen table, occasionally opening and closing the basement door just in case anybody got it into their head to try any funny business. This party was to be a bit different—more alcohol, less Seth Rogen, no parents—but Mom and Dad had no idea.

I'd been dating a sophomore saxophone player named Colin at the time, and was excited to spend some time with him in a dimly lit house with no parental supervision. Michelle had driven us there in her grandparents' minivan. She wasn't in band, but with her offbeat style, she fit in well. Besides, non-band kids who had a driver's license and access to their parents' vehicles were always welcome. Michelle was our designated driver, and the plan was to sleep over at her house after the party.

A few of the guys had managed to get some beer, and Shane had made it clear upon arrival that his father's liquor cabinet was off-limits. To me, that was the most unnecessary bit of information ever. I'd never drank alcohol in my life—never mind hard liquor—and certainly wasn't planning to steal any from a man whose day job involved the dissection of human bodies. I wasn't even planning on drinking at all. That was, until Colin decided to get into the hot tub and make-out with Brianna, a chatty freshman clarinet player. I was devastated, but didn't want to ruin everybody else's good time. Instead of asking Michelle to take me home, I went in search of Mr. Mitchell's liquor cabinet. Rumor had it that something called Kahlua was rather tasty.

I had no idea where the liquor cabinet actually was, so I wandered stealthily around the house, pretending to be looking for the bathroom. After covering the entire first floor, I made my way upstairs. I peeked into a few bedrooms, until I found, what looked to me, like a medical examiner's study. Blood-red heavy drapes. A huge mahogany desk in front of a wall of built-in bookcases, filled with impressive leather-bound books. Framed diplomas on the walls. A button-tufted leather couch with scroll arms. In the corner—and this was the clincher—was a model of a human skeleton dangling from a metal stand. Beside the skeleton was what had to be the liquor cabinet. Like the desk, it was huge and mahogany, and mercifully unlocked. I found a bottle of Kahlua right up front, unscrewed the cap—said a quick apology to Mr. Mitchell—and took a swig. Not bad. All those losers downstairs didn't know what they were missing. Especially Colin. Stupid Colin.

I flopped down onto the leather couch and took another sip. Then I reached my toe out and jiggled the legs of the hanging skeleton, making him dance. I started to giggle and took another swig of Kahlua. I liked it up there in Mr. Mitchell's study, alone and quiet. As an introvert, I was never very comfortable at parties. Whenever I did go to one, I ended up spending a lot of time recharging my social battery in the bathroom. I found Mr. Mitchell's study to be much more comfortable than any bathroom I'd ever been in, and I was very glad that I had found it. The more I drank, the more brazen I became with the skeleton, until eventually—what felt like an hour later—I was standing behind it, holding onto its arms, and making it do the Macarena.

"Dale a tu cuerpo alegría Macarena," I sang, really putting my hips into it.

"It is *always* the quiet ones," interrupted a voice from the hall.

I yelped and dropped the skeleton's arms, causing one of the wrists to fall off and clatter to the floor.

"Crap!" I picked it up and tried to jam it back into the arm bone. I missed completely, stumbled forward, and nearly knocked the entire thing over.

"Whoa, now," said Shane, darting into the room and grabbing the skeleton before it fell. He steadied it, and then looked from me to the half-empty bottle of Kahlua I had left on the floor. His eyebrows lifted in surprise. "I thought I said my dad's liquor cabinet was off-limits?"

"Did you?" I giggled. Then I burped. Then a wave of nausea hit me and I closed my eyes, swaying a bit. I felt Shane's hand on my lower back, the other one on my shoulder, as he slowly turned me around.

"Come on." He led me back over to the couch. I sat down next to him and flopped my head onto his shoulder. "Welcome to the world's most uncomfortable couch. What the heck happened to you, Cook?"

"Colin. Kissing...a stupid...freshman."

"Ah."

I opened my eyes, peering directly into Shane's neck. I was probably tickling him with my eyelashes, but he didn't move. It was unprecedented, us being so close like this. But in my current state, I liked it. It was warm, and comfortable, and I had nowhere else to be. I shifted my eyes from his neck, down toward his legs, where his left knee was jiggling. Up and down. Up and down.

"You nervous?" I asked. The jiggling stopped.

"Nope. You drunk?"

"Nope." I snorted. "Okay, yes. I just wanted get away from everybody. I can't believe he would do that to me."

"I can. Colin's an idiot."

"No, he's not." Even in my drunken, dumped state, I was still defending the guy. Force of habit, as this wasn't the first time Shane had made an insulting remark about him.

"Yes, he is. First off, he's a sophomore. Automatic idiot. Second of all..."

"Huh?" I jerked awake at the feel of being gently shaken.

"You fell asleep," said Shane.

"Oh." I tried to sit up, but Shane's arm was heavy around my shoulders. When had *that* happened? Not that I was bothered by it. Quite the opposite, actually. My cheek felt wet when I rested it back against his shoulder, and I noticed that I'd left a bit of drool on his sleeve. Nice. "What were you saying?"

"Never mind."

I suddenly wished that everybody else at this stupid party would disappear. Or that I could blink and be magically transported back home and into bed...but maybe with Shane's arm still around me. If there was one thing about this night that I didn't want to change, it was that.

"Hey," I said, suddenly realizing something. "How come your breath doesn't smell like beer?"

"Haven't had any."

"How come? It's *your* party."

I felt him shrug against my cheek. "I guess I prefer to watch everyone else act like idiots."

"You think I'm an idiot?" I murmured, an unexpected wave of

73

shame coming over me. Honestly, what had I been thinking? My parents were going to kill me if they found out I'd been drinking. If relationships were based on IQ, Colin and I probably deserved each other.

"Let's see, everyone else is downstairs trying to bounce Ping-Pong balls into plastic cups. You were up here making a skeleton do the Macarena. You're not an idiot, Caity. You're awesome."

"I don't feel so awesome," I groaned, shifting on the stiff couch and lifting my head. Bad idea. The room started to spin. "Talk to me about something else, quick."

"Like what?"

My eyes moved from the skeleton, to a 3D cutaway of the human brain I'd just noticed on the corner of Mr. Mitchell's desk. "Like this medical examiner's convention. What's it like? Stodgy old doctors taking notes in one of those surgical amphitheaters? Lots of blood and guts?" My stomach turned over at the words *blood and guts*.

Shane laughed. "It's actually held at a Marriott in San Diego. My mom said there's a tiki theme and an open bar. And tomorrow they're going to Sea World."

"You're kidding?"

"Nope. Last year it was held in Orlando and they all went to Disney. Look." He pulled out his phone and brought up a photo of his parents standing with a group of smiling people in front of Cinderella's Castle.

"You've blown my mind, Mitchell," I said. "Thanks."

"Any time."

I closed my eyes again, but something wasn't right. I wasn't thinking about blood and guts anymore, but my stomach still felt a bit warm. Like I'd eaten a big bowl of beef stew right before riding Space Mountain.

"Um, Shane?"

"Yeah?"

Pushing one hand into his stomach and propelling myself off

the couch, I ran out into the hallway. Crap. When I'd been poking around earlier, I'd managed to find every room in the house except for the bathroom.

"Second door on the left!" shouted Shane.

Grateful, I darted into the bathroom, knelt down in front of the toilet, and threw up. I rested my head on my elbow on the edge of the toilet seat. I could hear the party still going on full swing downstairs, a world away. I wondered for a moment what Colin was doing, and if he'd even noticed that I'd disappeared. Shane came in then, pulled my hair back into a ponytail, and tore off some toilet paper with his other hand.

"Here."

I held up one finger, vomited again, then took the toilet paper and wiped my mouth. "Thanks." If I hadn't looked like an idiot before, I certainly did now.

When I was certain nothing more was going to come out, Shane filled me a glass of water, ordered me to drink all of it, and then walked me back into his father's study. I lay down on the couch and he covered me with a blanket.

"My dad brought this home from the morgue," he whispered.

I flung the blanket to the floor and sat bolt upright.

"Kidding!" He laughed. "It's from Target. Relax."

"I hate you," I mumbled, settling back down and closing my eyes. It really was the world's most uncomfortable couch.

"You love me," he mumbled back.

I smiled and rolled over to face the back of the couch, listening to the creak of the floorboards as he walked back toward the hall. I wished for a moment that he would stay. But it was his party, and people would notice if he'd disappeared. Unlike me and stupid Colin. I really *was* an idiot.

"We all have our moments," said Shane quietly, from across the room, as if he'd read my mind. Then the door clicked shut and I drifted off to sleep.

When I woke, it was morning.

The house was quiet and my mouth felt all fuzzy. I was face-down, with a pounding headache, and my head hanging halfway off the couch. With a groan, I opened my eyes, and jumped. On the floor beside the couch, staring up at me, was Mr. Mitchell's model skeleton. It was dressed in a Hollister T-shirt and a pair of plaid cargo shorts. A note was pinned to its chest.

Caity –

Michelle said your parents weren't expecting you home so I let you stay. You've been asleep for eighty years. I kept you company until I died and the flesh rotted off my bones. Hope you're happy. Coffee and donuts in the kitchen.

- Shane

P.S. Not actually dead. Will drive you home when ready.

CHAPTER 11

I wasn't prepared for what I saw when we pulled up in front of the house. The Mitchell's grand, old Colonial had been completely done-up in thousands upon thousands of Christmas lights. Each of the trees on the front lawn had been expertly, and painstakingly, wrapped in colorful lights, from the branches all the way down to the bottom of each trunk. There was an inflatable snow globe, a family of twinkling penguins, a couple of polar bears, several elves, and the words *Seasons Greetings* spelled out in six-foot tall, lighted letters. The walkway to the house was lined with flashing lollipops, and the row of tall, skinny trees separating Shane's property from the property next door had been transformed into a row of red and white candy cane sticks at least thirty feet high. Cars were parked up and down the street, and children and families were milling about on the lawn. I rolled down the window and heard holiday music.

"This is bananas," I said to Dad.

"It certainly is something," he replied.

I rolled the window back up and turned to look at him. "And you're telling me *Shane* did this?"

"Yup. Past two years. There's a crowd here every night."

"Does somebody help him?" Shane didn't have any siblings, and I couldn't imagine any of his old high school buddies having the patience for this sort of thing. I couldn't imagine Shane having the patience for this sort of thing.

"Nope. He always starts way back in September. I see him out here all the time, up on that ladder."

"But he can't possibly be out here all the time. He has band stuff every weekend until Thanksgiving!"

Dad shrugged, and I took out my phone.

When did you turn into Clark Griswold?? I typed. Then I added the emoji with the blushing cheeks and the eyes bugging out. About five seconds later, the front door to the house opened and out came Shane. He was wearing a hooded sweatshirt and jeans, and looked around at all the cars until he spotted Dad's Harvester. He jogged across the lawn as I jumped out of the truck.

"You *did* this?" I shouted, before he had even reached us.

"Yeah!" he shouted back.

"This is amazing!" I gushed. "Isn't this amazing?" I looked around at my family.

"It's lovely," said Mom, who had pulled up behind Dad's truck and joined us on the lawn. I could tell that she was trying to look enthusiastic, but must have already seen this a million times. Nate hadn't even bothered to get out of the car. I could see him in the passenger seat, staring at his phone with his headphones on.

"You want the grand tour?" asked Shane.

"Sure!" I looked at Mom and Dad.

"You go ahead," said Mom. "We'll wait here." Even in the dark, I could see the meaningful look she gave me, and the fact that she had not so subtly elbowed Dad in the ribs. But I didn't care. Not even my ex-boyfriend, Ben, and his snowy Vermont sleigh rides could compete with the Christmas magic happening right here on Shane's front lawn. I tagged happily along behind him as he started off toward the house, turning in circles as I walked, trying to absorb all the details.

"How many lights do you put up?" I asked.

"Over a hundred thousand."

"No way!"

"You want to count? I'll go get my ladder."

"No," I laughed. "I believe you. Oh, and there's Santa!"

Up by the chimney, an illuminated, robotic Santa waved his hand. Back and forth. Back and forth. The entire roof beneath his feet was decorated in a diamond pattern of flashing, chasing lights. I stood there staring up at the house, transfixed, until Shane grabbed me by the hand. I turned away from Santa and looked up into Shane's eyes. He looked a bit ghostly standing there with all the flashing, colored lights reflecting off his face. But his eyes looked blue, and warm, and happy. I could tell he was delighted that I was in such awe of his hard work. I lightly squeezed his hand, which was still warm from having been indoors. I wondered what he'd been doing in there before we'd arrived, all alone in such a big house.

"Come on," he said softly, leading me around to the other side of the house.

My heart beat rapidly. We had a bit of a history with sides of houses. But this wasn't the summer after high school and we weren't seventeen. Shane hadn't just blindsided me with the news that he loved me. Even so, the memory was fresh in my mind, and I wondered what I would do if he were to come to a screeching halt in the middle of his yard and say those words to me again. *I think I'm in love with you, Caity.* Would I take off to Boston again? With my commitment to Miss Annabeth and the Christmas show, I couldn't do that until after the holidays. Since I had to stay, would I give us a chance? That still only gave us a matter of weeks, which didn't seem like nearly enough time for any sort of second chance to take root. Eight years later and our timing was still terrible.

I took a deep breath as we rounded the side of the house. Long strands of white lights formed a large circle as they ran from the ground to the top of a metal pole, at least twenty feet high. An enormous star, probably intended for a Christmas tree display in a town square, sat at the top. Shane pulled me into the center of the circle.

"Holy moly," I breathed, looking up. Shane let go of my hand so I could turn around slowly. I felt like I was in another world, surrounded by stars. I stopped spinning and looked him seriously in the eye. "People must come from everywhere to see this!"

He shrugged. "I get some traffic."

"My father says there's a crowd here every night."

"All right, yeah. I'm kind of a big deal."

"You should be charging people money to see this!"

"Well, it's a public road....so...I'd have to put up a pretty big curtain."

"You know what I mean," I said, laughing. "This is amazing, Shane. When do you even have time to put all this up?"

He jammed his hands into the pockets of his sweatshirt and looked across the lawn to the house. "After work. Weekends after practices. It keeps me occupied during the holidays. Takes my mind off being alone in that big, old house."

I narrowed my eyes. "Are you telling me that you have no life?"

Shane laughed. "I've always wondered if there was a name for it. Thank you, Caity."

"No offense," I said, walking toward the outer edge of the circle. "I'm just surprised that Shane Took-Three-Different-Girls-to-the-Carnival-Three-Nights-in-a-Row Mitchell no longer has a life. No girlfriend? It's preposterous." Butterflies took flight in my stomach as I so cleverly probed for information.

"No girlfriend," said Shane, shaking his head. "Nothing serious since I've moved back to Reindeer Falls."

"What about all the girls we went to high school with?" I

80

asked, crinkling my nose. "They must've loved it when you came back. It was probably on the front page of the *Gazette*."

"I had a few dates, sure. You remember Brianna, right?"

My heart stopped at the name, and I turned around slowly.

"Kidding!" he said, holding his hands out to catch the daggers.

"Not funny."

"Sorry. Whatever happened to Colin, anyway?"

"No clue." I shrugged. "And stop changing the subject."

"What was the subject again?"

"You not having a life. How is that possible?"

He scrubbed his hand through his hair. "What can I say? Sometimes I'd rather just string Christmas lights than go through the trouble of dating. It's pretty peaceful up there, alone on a ladder."

I raised my eyebrows. "The same person who couldn't last a single bus ride without chatting it up, actually *enjoys* some alone time now?"

"The art of enjoying your own company," he said. "I get it now. It's a skill you had long before the rest of us. I should probably apologize again for bugging you so much on those bus rides. You probably just wanted to read, huh?"

"Yep." I said. Then I smiled and batted a hand at him. "But it was worth it."

"It was," said Shane, a smile tugging at the corner of his mouth as his eyes searched my face.

There had always been an inherent kindness about Shane. There was a big heart behind those good looks and charm, and that big heart was the reason I'd never put up much of a fight when he tried to chat with me on the bus. That kindness seemed to have grown deeper over the years, while some of the things I had found less appealing—his revolving door of girlfriends, for one—seemed to have lessened. It was a dangerously pleasant realization.

"So, um, do you still have your dad's creepy skeleton?" I asked, changing the subject. "Or did he bring it with him to Florida?"

"Oh, I still have it. You want to come in and say hello? Check out the Kahlua supply? My dad left his liquor cabinet behind, too."

I shivered slightly at the thought of going into that house. Of Shane leading me upstairs. Thankfully, my family was waiting for me and I couldn't stay.

"It's tempting," I said. "But I haven't had the stomach for Kahlua in about nine years. I should probably get going, anyway."

"Right," said Shane. "I'll walk you back."

We were halfway across the lawn when Shane stopped short. I stopped too, and turned around to face him.

"What's up?" I asked. He was looking off into the distance, in the direction of Dad's truck, just like he had all those years ago in front of my house. I noticed my hands were suddenly shaking and my mouth had gone dry. A car drove past and tooted its horn, making the both of us jump. Shane glanced after it, and then back at me.

"Do you um, want to, maybe, do something one of these nights?" he asked. "Like...dinner?"

"Like...a date?" I asked, cautiously, as "Joy to the World" started playing over the speaker system.

"Like a date."

"Wow," I said. "If I hadn't just found out how desperate you were for dates, I might have been flattered." I bit my lip.

Shane took a step closer, his blue eyes boring into me. "I never said I was *desperate* for dates, Caitlin. I just said that I'd rather string Christmas lights. But now that *you're* back, everything's changed."

Wow. Okay. Forty-something degrees outside and I was starting to sweat. If Mom and Dad didn't have their faces plastered up against the car windows, who knows what I might have done. Eight years suddenly seemed much too long since our first and only kiss. An overwhelming longing welled up inside of me and I reached out and playfully jiggled the zipper pull on his sweatshirt. There wasn't much else I could do that Mom and Dad wouldn't notice. What I really wanted to do would have had more than one car tooting its horn.

"Okay then," I agreed, swallowing hard. "A date." I looked up at him and smiled, letting my hand drop from the zipper.

"Finally," muttered Shane, smiling.

"Finally," I repeated. I took a few steps toward the street. "So, um...call me. *You* call *me.*"

I pointed from Shane to myself, then turned and ran the rest of the way to the truck. I jumped in beside my dad and slammed the door, like I was seventeen and in high school all over again.

CHAPTER 12

"*There* she is, Miss America!"

"*Please* stop," said Emma, turning bright red as she stood up from her table in the back corner of Holly's. She came toward me and pulled me into a hug.

I squeezed her back, laughing. "I couldn't resist. You look great!"

"Oh, please." She took a step back and looked me up and down, shaking her head. "*You* look great. You late bloomers are so lucky. It's like you're still eighteen."

"This coming from a supermodel?"

"Oh, Caity," Emma groaned. "We have a lot to catch up on. It's been much too long."

"Way too long. You're living in a *barn*?"

Emma closed her eyes and pinched the bridge of her nose. "*Above* a barn. I'll explain. But first—"

"Refill?" I picked her big, empty coffee mug up off the table.

"Please."

I stepped into line behind Milton Picklebarrel. Milton was one of those people you thought were old back when you were a kid, yet they somehow still walk the earth. I waited patiently while he paid for his coffee with about a thousand pennies, glancing back occasionally at my old friend. I'd given Emma a call first thing this morning about getting together. The two of us couldn't have been more opposite back in high school. It wasn't as noticeable when we'd first met in sixth grade at the community center—a mutual interest in weaving friendship bracelets had been enough for us to form a bond. But by the time we got to high school, the cheerleader and the band geek didn't always have the opportunity to spend much time together.

I would wave to her during football games—me in the stands with my flute and my polyester uniform, Emma on the sidelines doing high kicks in a short skirt. In school, we ate lunch at separate tables, and went to parties thrown by different groups of kids. But we still passed notes in the hallway, and every time Emma had broken up with a boyfriend, it wasn't her fellow cheerleaders that she turned to for support, it was me. I was the listener.

Emma always said that she was jealous of my musical ability. She said she wished she had learned to play an instrument because it would have come in handy during her beauty pageants. I always told her that I wished I had her flexibility because it would come in handy on my honeymoon. Similar to Shane, she always laughed when I said things like that. She said she found it *delightfully shocking* when inappropriate things came out of my innocent mouth.

After a good five minutes had passed, I peered over Milton's shoulder. He didn't seem to have quite enough pennies, and the girl working at the register seemed to be running out of patience.

"Here you go, Mr. Picklebarrel," I said, pulling a few bills out of my wallet. "It's on me."

"Oh, my. Thank you, thank you," he said, slowly turning around and arching one bushy eyebrow at me. "Veronica?"

"Caitlin," I said, loudly. "Caitlin Cook. You probably don't remember me. I used to live here in Reindeer Falls."

"Veronica, yes! I have your cat!" He pointed one finger up in the air. "A fat old tabby. I'll call your mother to sort it all out."

"Perfect," I said. "Enjoy your coffee."

"Thank you, darling." He scooped his pennies into his hand, poured them back into one of his large, droopy pockets, then shuffled off toward the door.

"Was that Milton Picklebarrel?" asked Emma, after I'd brought our coffees back to the table.

"Yup."

"Wow. He's still kickin', huh?"

"Still kickin', and he thinks he has my cat. Well, Veronica's cat."

"Who?"

"Never mind." I rested my coffee cup in the tiny space between Emma's laptop and a stack of resumes. Then I picked one up and started skimming through it. "Impressive resume, Em. But where are your headshots?" I turned the paper over as if I expected to find one on the back.

Emma sighed. "I'm not looking for the sort of job that requires a headshot."

"Why not?" I frowned. "What happened?"

She motioned to her face and her body, both of which looked perfectly lovely to me. "*This* happened."

"What? You got fantastic boobs and a face like Lily James?"

"I got *old*, Caity."

"We're the same age, Em."

"Okay, maybe not real world old, but *modeling* old. And I gained a few pounds. And don't even talk to me about my boobs...they're not where they used to be."

I bent over and looked underneath the table. "Oh, yeah. There they are."

Emma laughed and gave me a gentle kick. "I missed you, Caity. If I weren't so depressed about my career and poor Miss Annabeth, I'd be pretty happy to see you right now."

"You know, my mom said something similar the other day. She said that even if I was home because I'd lost my job, and my boyfriend, and because my favorite teacher was ill, that she was still happy to see me. I guess my mom loves me more than you do." I stuck out my tongue.

Emma took a sip of coffee and mulled the idea around in her head. "Okay, yeah. Despite it all, I *am* still happy to see you. Take that, Mrs. Cook."

"I'm happy to see you, too. Even if it's because you've gotten old and fat."

We clinked coffee mugs.

"So, are you back for good?" I asked. "No more New York? And why the *barn*?"

"I'm back for the foreseeable future, yes. I've just been feeling so tired of New York lately. I think I'm ready to figure out what's next. As for the barn...I don't know. I'd just gotten back into town, with no idea where I was going to stay, and then I saw the ad for the room in the window of The Greasy Antler. It sounded so opposite my life in New York, you know? So country. So rustic. I've been craving rustic, Caity."

"To rustic!" I said, holding my mug in the air so we could clink again.

"And Mrs. Clemson's a sweetheart," she continued, "but I'm pretty sure she thinks I'm trying to seduce her fifteen-year-old son. You leave your barn shade up *one time*..."

"No need to elaborate."

"Anyway," said Emma, clearing her throat. "Eventually I'll have to move out of the barn. But I can't really afford to do that until I find myself a job."

"I saw a Help Wanted sign in the window of the bookstore the other day," I suggested.

"A bookstore?" asked Emma, scrunching up her nose. "That seems more like your sort of thing. What do I know about selling books?"

"They're just words on paper, Em. They practically sell themselves."

"Maybe I'll check it out," she said, staring forlornly at the wall behind me and taking a long sip of coffee. "How did it even come to this?"

"I don't know," I said. "But I'm unemployed, too. And my boyfriend was cheating on me. And I'm living in my childhood bedroom, surrounded by my parents' ever-increasing hoard of antiques. So, don't go thinking you're the only one suffering."

Emma put her face in her hands. "I feel bad complaining about our lives, when it's poor Miss Annabeth who's genuinely suffering."

"You're right," I sighed. "I can't even imagine what she's going through, trying to tie up all her loose ends in case a donor doesn't come through. And on top of that, knowing that the community center is going to close. It's more depressing than anything the two of us have going on."

"I know. I keep trying to think of something I can do to help raise money, but I'm out of ideas. I guess all we can do is perform our little song and make one of her wishes come true. She never did ask us for money. Just for the song."

"She would *never* ask us for money, even if we had it," I said. "It's so unfair. We made so many memories at that place. When I was lonely my first semester at Harvard, those memories are what got me through. I thought about how hard it had been for me to make friends, and what a miracle it was that I ended up with two such great ones. It was all thanks to her."

"And now she's brought us back," said Emma, dramatically shrugging her shoulders almost up to her ears. "It's all very Hallmark Channel, isn't it?"

"A town called Reindeer Falls? Who would've thought?"

"Let's see, if we were in a made-for-TV movie, Santa would be ordering a latte right about now, secretly seeking out his next wife." Emma eyed each of the customers in the coffee shop.

"I never really understood the appeal of marrying Santa," I said, crinkling my nose.

"He's a powerful man. He could whisk you away to a magical place and make all your wishes come true."

"Yes, but that magical place would be *freezing*. And just because he's powerful, that means a woman should tie herself down to an elderly elf with a milk and cookies gut? I'm telling you, women haven't thought this thing all the way through."

"Only *you* would think it all the way through," laughed Emma. "By the way, speaking of Christmas, Tammy Pulaski said she saw you hanging out on Shane Mitchell's front lawn last night. Can I confirm?"

My jaw dropped, and I suddenly remembered the car that had driven by, honking its horn. "Geez, I forgot what it was like living in a small town."

"Well, now you've remembered. Spill."

"There's nothing to *spill*." I filled her in on the details of what had gone down between Shane and me since I'd been back, concluding with the fact that he'd asked me out on a date. "It's nothing, though. Just dinner and catching up. I'm going back to Boston after Christmas. So... it's nothing." I thought of the feel of Shane's hand in mine as we ran across the lawn, and the upcoming promise of an entire evening together. *Nothing* was not even remotely the correct word to describe it.

Emma sighed. "You two were straight out of a movie. The dorky girl who gets taken to prom by the hot guy. She lets down her hair and takes off her glasses and it turns out she's been a babe all along."

"Thank you, Em. But Shane and I never went to prom together. And he was in band too, remember? He wasn't exactly Tom Brady."

Emma whistled. "News flash, Caity. Shane was a hottie. Still is. You are such a Yankee, by the way. *Tom Brady*. We've got to get you back home to the South, pronto."

"Says the girl who's spent the last eight years living in New York?"

"Touché," she laughed. "But seriously, if you don't go running off back to Boston, I predict you and Shane will be picking out curtains for that big, old house of his by New Year's."

We stared each other down—Emma slowly nodding her head up and down, and me slowly shaking mine from side to side—until we both started laughing.

"I am glad to be home," I said. "But it's only temporary. My life is in Boston."

"Your life should be with the people who love you. Your family. *Me*, now that I'm stuck here. Maybe even Shane."

"Shane loved me back in high school, Em. Eight years ago. He can't possibly still feel that way."

"But don't you want to find out?" she asked. "A second chance was dropped right into your lap, and now you want to leave again? At least last time you had a good reason. This time, what are you leaving for? To do the same thing I'm doing"—she motioned to her laptop and the stack of resumes— "only a thousand miles away, alone in an apartment that you can't afford?"

I rolled my eyes and stared out the window. It had been easier to deny the appeal of moving back to Reindeer Falls when I was in Boston, not sitting here in a café with my best friend.

"Just think about it, Caity. Okay?" Emma reached across the table and squeezed my hand.

"Okay," I said, softening and squeezing hers back.

At the sound of jingling bells, we both turned toward the door and started to laugh. A man in a full Santa suit had just walked in, and was ordering himself a latte.

CHAPTER 13

*I*t had been a couple of days since I'd stopped by Shane's house to see the lights, and I still hadn't heard from him about arranging our date. I didn't know if he was trying to make some sort of passive-aggressive point about the way I'd treated him after I left for college, or if he'd recently borrowed a copy of *The Rules* from the Reindeer Falls town library and was waiting out the requisite seventy-two hours. Whatever it was, I was trying not to stress about it. I had plenty to keep me busy at home. Now that Nate's room was clean, and a Christmas tree was up in the living room, I decided to focus a bit on my bedroom.

It wasn't fair to Mom and Dad that I had never bothered coming home long enough to clean out my things; especially since I knew they would never get around to doing it for me. If I had, they probably wouldn't have felt the need to take over Nate's room. Still, there was a part of me that didn't want to give up my one remaining square of real estate in Reindeer Falls. If I relinquished my childhood bedroom, I'd have nothing left. There wouldn't even be a place for me to sleep when I came back to visit.

Now that I was home—helping my family, helping Miss Annabeth, and once again on speaking terms with Shane—the thought of periodically coming back to visit didn't seem so bad. What was starting to seem worse was the thought of returning to Boston where I had no job, no boyfriend and, to be honest, not many girlfriends either. Making friends had never come easily to me. If it weren't for Miss Annabeth dragging the three of us outside that night and tying those bracelets onto our wrists, who knows how I would have ended up? But with those girls around me, I always felt secure.

With Emma and Michelle, I thought that I was set for life. I'd always imagined us as grownups, taking each other's kids to ballet lessons and soccer practice. I thought the three of us would end up taking our kids trick-or-treating together, and going on summer vacations to the mountains. Then we all went our separate ways—spread out around the country—and I was right back to square one. I found myself all alone at Harvard, surrounded by my bubbly, outgoing peers.

How come you're so quiet?

Someone had actually asked me that during the first week of classes. Some boorish dolt, who had obviously blackmailed the admissions office in order to get in, had been sitting in the row behind me. I jumped as he leaned forward and spoke the words directly into my ear, invading my personal space. *Why are you so quiet?* Asking him in return why he was so lame didn't seem appropriate at the college level, so I simply shrugged and went back to flipping through my notes. It seemed I would never escape the questions about why I am the way I am.

What I'd really wanted to do was turn around and shout, *Who do you expect me to be talking to? I haven't made a friend on this entire campus!* I was fascinated by people who had the ability to make friends quickly. I watched them chitchat before class, wondering what they could possibly be talking about, and how they managed to keep the conversation going for so long. Such an endless stream of words would leave me exhausted. It was at those times that I missed my Reindeer Falls friends the most. The way the three of us had been so different, yet understood each other perfectly. The way we could just be together without always having to gab. The way I didn't have any fear that they found me odd.

I also thought of Shane and the easy way we'd had with each other. Sure, he'd asked me why I was so quiet that first time on the bus, but he'd been sure to never do it again. He'd even told me once, on a particularly dull drive through Kentucky, that he was somewhat in awe of me. *Awe?* I'd repeated. *I've never met anyone with so much going on beneath the surface,* he'd replied. Perhaps the boorish dolt sitting behind me had been another Shane in the making, if only I'd had the energy to give him a chance. Somehow, I doubted it. There was only one Shane Mitchell in the world, and I'd left him far behind.

I grabbed the plastic box full of folded notes off my desk and sat down on the floor. This would be an easy thing to start with. I'd read through them, have a laugh, and off they'd go to the recycle bin. I smiled as I read them, picturing all of our old teachers and classmates, rolling my eyes at all of the pointless drama. Even though the notes were just as immature and predictable as I'd expected, I found myself re-folding them and stashing them back into the box. Maybe it was a result of my hoarding genes, but I couldn't bring myself to throw them away. Those notes were like time capsules. Pieces of history. Those notes didn't exactly belong in the Smithsonian, but they meant something to *me.*

I picked up another one. This one was a little different, as it had no writing on the front. As I unfolded it, I realized that there was nothing written inside it either. Instead, a pink and purple friendship bracelet fell out. It was the bracelet that Miss Annabeth had tied onto my wrist all those years ago.

Friendship is a precious thing. It's made and woven out of strings.

The kind of ties that can't be seen. But last in life through everything.

The words echoed in my head as I remembered sliding the bracelet off my hand the night before leaving for Harvard. My wrist had looked so bare without it, but I'd felt too silly wearing such a childish thing to college. So I had taken it off, folded it into a piece of notebook paper, and tossed it into the box. I squeezed my fingers together and slid it back over my hand and onto my wrist. It still fit.

As I went back to flicking through notes, one in particular caught my eye. *To: Caitlin,* it said simply on the front. It was thick and the handwriting was different from the rest. There were no hearts over the I's or flowers dotting the corners. I opened it up to find a note that Shane had written to me, neatly dated in the top right-hand corner. Sophomore year. I smiled as I scanned down the page, and then read through the two additional pages behind it, butterflies fluttering to life in my stomach. So many times over the past eight years these words had also echoed in my head. It wasn't actually a *note* that Shane had written me...it was a song.

It was a song that he had written on one very long bus ride home from Nashville. Shane's girlfriend had made Jeff Murray, the trombone player, swap seats with her because she was mad at Shane and wanted to sit by herself to stare moodily out the window. We were an hour into the trip when Shane got up and asked my seatmate, Christina Swanson, to swap with *him*, but she refused, claiming that Jeff had a body odor problem—something that none of us in good conscience could argue against. Shane returned to the back of the bus, where the occasional glance over the seats found him holding his breath and scribbling furiously into a notebook for the next two hours. What I was looking at was the end result.

A Rose on Fire
We're taking the black highway
to our gray hometown

the yellow bus is humming
the pink sun is going down

BUT THE ONLY sunset
   I happen to see
   is the fiery red hair
   in the seat in front of me

RED LIKE AN APPLE
   or a cardinal flying higher
   Red like a rose,
   like a rose on fire
   Red like a Corvette
   with flames and burning tires
   Red like a rose,
   like a rose on fire

THE SILVER MOON is rising
   but all I want to see
   is the fiery red hair
   in the seat next to me

RED LIKE AN APPLE
   or a cardinal flying higher
   Red like a rose,
   like a rose on fire
   Red like a Corvette
   with flames and burning tires
   Red like a rose,
   like a rose on fire

. . .

HE'D SLIPPED me the folded pages, without a word, as we filed off the bus. It was quite some time before I was back home and able to read it in the privacy of my bedroom. I'd been expecting a long list of inappropriate questions that he hadn't been able to ask me on the bus. Instead, I found a love song. I didn't know what to think, yet my mind had raced all night, and I didn't get much sleep. Come Monday morning at school, however, it was business as usual between us. Shane and his girlfriend had made up, and there were no further hints at a burning, unrequited love. No more roses on fire. Confused, and angry with myself for losing sleep over Shane Mitchell, I'd folded up the song and tossed it into the box.

I was still rereading the lyrics when my cell phone rang. Shane. Figures.

"Hey," I said, trying to sound casual. "What's up?"

"I was just thinking about what you said the other night. About people paying to see my Christmas lights? Did you really mean that?"

"Yeah," I said, folding up the song pages and putting them back into the box. "I mean, I don't think you could actually *force* anybody to pay. Like you said, it's a public road. Maybe voluntarily, though. Like a donation."

"A donation. That's what I was thinking. The community center needs money, right?"

"Right."

"Well, what if next weekend I had Santa at my house to greet the kids? And maybe somebody dressed as Clip-Clop?"

I snort-laughed. "I can't believe you remembered my name for him."

"I accidentally called him that once, in front of my students. They tease me about it relentlessly now, thank you very much. Anyway, I was thinking I could serve hot chocolate and cookies, and everybody would be welcome to come by free of charge, but a small donation to the community center would be appreciated."

"That's brilliant."

"You think?"

"Yes! But who's going to dress up as Santa?"

"Me, of course. I rented the suit yesterday. I tried it on and wore it into Holly's for kicks. Nobody even recognized me."

"That was *you?*" I started coughing.

"I would have come over to say hi, except that Emma was with you. I didn't want her making fun of me."

"Let me get this straight," I said, sitting down on the bed. "You were embarrassed for Emma to recognize you, but now you're going to invite the entire town to your house where you're planning to walk around, saying *ho ho ho,* in a Santa suit?"

"That's right."

"Well, I know that *I* would definitely pay to see that."

"Oh, you'll see it," said Shane. "You're going to be right there with me."

"Excuse me?"

"Every Santa needs a Mrs. Claus."

"Oh, no."

"Hang on a sec."

I heard the faint jingling of bells, some shuffling, and the sound of muffled voices. Then, much more clearly because he was purposely speaking directly into the phone, "Good morning, Sandy. Do you still have that green velvet dress for sale? The one with the lacy collar?"

"No!" I shouted. "Don't you dare!"

Now I could hear Mom's voice responding in the distance. "Of course, love! We can't seem to get rid of that thing!"

"Well, today's your lucky day. I'll take it!"

"Don't sell it to him!" I shouted into the phone. "Mom! Can you hear me? Do *not* sell him that dress!"

"What in the world is that racket?" asked Mom. "Is someone

yelling at you?"

"Wrong number," said Shane, and then loudly into the phone, *"No hablo Ingles!"*

I listened—silently fuming—to the entire credit card transaction, and then to the sound of the jingling of bells again as he exited the shop. I was about to say something rude, when the thought of Shane standing there on Main Street holding a big, poufy green dress in his arms made me choke back a laugh.

"Should I stop by Walmart or do you think you can provide your own curly white wig?" he asked.

"I hate you."

"You love me. So, Sunday night, six o'clock. I've already started putting flyers around town. I don't know about you, but I think I came up with best first date idea *ever*."

"That's our *date?* You said we were going out to dinner."

"We are. We'll do the North Pole reenactment first, and then it's off to dinner. Anywhere you like. Deal?"

"We're changing clothes first, right?" It seemed obvious, but with Shane you never knew.

"There'd probably be a free meal in it for us if Santa and Mrs. Claus were to show up at Applebee's the week before Christmas."

"Shane."

"Okay, okay. We change clothes first. Deal?"

"Deal."

I looked at myself in the bedroom mirror, shaking my head. I couldn't believe I'd just agreed to dress up like an amusement park employee and freeze my buns off on Shane's front lawn. Still, I could have easily refused to do it, and I hadn't. Just as I could have thrown Shane's song into the trash eight years ago, but hadn't. Part of me realized that this was actually a good idea, and a great way to raise money for the community center. Part of me was willing to suffer through the humiliation of dressing up as Mrs. Claus in order to help out the ones I loved.

To be honest, part of me could hardly wait.

CHAPTER 14

"*Y*ou know, back in Boston I have about twenty different malls to choose from. And they're all way closer than this one."

Nate took a sip of the iced coffee that we'd bought forty-five minutes ago in Gatlinburg, and shrugged. "Yeah, but can you afford to buy anything? Remember the last time we came out to visit? Dad almost lost it at Starbucks."

"Good point," I laughed, exiting the highway and pulling onto the mall access road. Then, in my best Dad voice, *"Five dollars for a coffee? I could buy a week's worth of groceries for five dollars!* When do you think was the last time Dad went grocery shopping?"

"Early nineteen hundreds, apparently."

I'd borrowed Mom's car and picked Nate up after school so that we could do some Christmas shopping at the big mall in Knoxville. We'd agreed to each chip in and buy Mom and Dad joint gifts from the both of us. I felt slightly guilty being the older sister and not offering to put in a larger dollar amount, but I had no job and I had rent to pay. Nate worked part-time at Christmas Past and had zero bills to pay. I also had no idea what sort of gifts to get them, so I was hoping that Nate could clue me in.

"Oh, wow," I breathed, pulling into the parking lot. I hadn't been to this mall since high school, and even then, the hour-long drive made it a rare occurrence. "It looks exactly the same. Sears. Dillard's. No Nordstrom?"

"I really hope you're joking," said Nate. "But, if you're up for driving a few more hours, there's probably one in Nashville."

"Um, no," I said, turning off the engine and getting out of the car. "What would Mom and Dad possibly need from Nordstrom, anyway?"

Nate got out the passenger side and looked at me over the roof. "What do Mom and Dad need from *here*?"

"Don't say that."

"What?"

"We just drove for an hour! Don't say there's nothing here that they need! I thought you had a plan!"

Nate looked at me like I was nuts. "I never said I had a plan. You said you wanted to go shopping. And unless you want to buy them books, yarn, or scratch-off lottery tickets from the booming metropolis that is Main Street, Reindeer Falls, then this here is the place to go." He waved his hand toward the mall. "Besides, I figured *you* had some sort of plan."

"I guess we're browsing, then," I said, rolling my eyes. "Come on. We'll find something."

I marched off toward the main entrance, with Nate trailing along behind me. We'd walked about a quarter of a way through the mall when I glanced back and noticed he had his earbuds in. "Hey, take those out!"

"Why?"

"Because I've been talking to you this whole time! I thought you weren't responding because you're a moody teenager. Turns out you haven't heard a word I said."

"I heard you. I just needed a break."

"You're the only person who's ever implied I talk too much." I punched him on the arm. "Come on, Nate. I don't want to talk *at* you. I want to talk *with* you. Interact. Spend some quality time with my little brother. We haven't spent this much time together in years."

He reluctantly pulled out the earbuds and shoved them into his coat pocket. "Ever."

"Huh?"

"We haven't spent this much time together *ever*. I was eight years old when you went off to college. I was like, in diapers."

I stopped in my tracks, spun around, and put my hand on his chest so that he'd stop walking, too. "You were *eight?*"

I didn't know why the news came as such a shock. I knew Nate had been eight years old when I left. He'd been entering second grade the same year that I entered Harvard. For our entire lives we had existed in two completely different worlds, and it had never seemed more evident than when I had graduated from high school. I was an adult, or so I'd thought, with a life and issues and responsibilities. Nate was just a kid, with toys and snacks and stuffed animals. I'd kept my distance, with barely a second thought, for most of his childhood. I watched him grow up via photographs that Mom would occasionally email to me at school. Mom and Dad had taken Nate to Disney World the summer he turned nine, and they asked me to come, too. But I'd already been—Mom and Dad had taken me twice before Nate was even born—and I wasn't interested. It also happened to be my first summer home from college, and I had the prospect of an awkward confrontation with Shane still looming over me. When the opportunity came along to instead spend the summer studying abroad in Spain, I jumped at the chance.

And so it went throughout the years—coming home for a weekend here and there, barely interacting with a preteen Nate. Noticing in silence that my parents' hoarding was getting increasingly worse, and being tremendously relieved when I was able to leave again. I didn't think there was anything I could do to fix it, and I didn't have the patience to want to try. Not back then.

But looking at Nate now, I wondered if he felt like he had been an only child. Did he feel like I had abandoned him? He wasn't my responsibility, though. If he grew up in a disaster of a house, that was on Mom and Dad. Wasn't it? Still, he was no longer the eight-year-old kid that my teenaged self was willing to ignore. He was nearly a grown man now, and I could sense that he had a whole lot of issues going on inside his head. I wanted to blame them all on Mom and Dad, but I knew better. I could have been there for him. I could have been a better older sister.

I wanted to talk to him seriously about all of this, but standing in front of Bath & Body Works, enveloped in a cloud of holiday body sprays, didn't seem like the time or place. I started walking again, and he followed.

"So... should we try Sears?" I asked. "Mom and Dad seem like Sears people."

"Works for me," said Nate. "I'm thinking a new hooded sweat-shirt for Mom, and some sort of tool for Dad."

"Okay. What kind of tool? Like, a hammer?"

Nate shook his head. "He already has a lot of hammers."

"How about a wrench?"

"Tons of them."

"Screwdriver?"

"We're going to get Dad a screwdriver for Christmas?"

"How's that any worse than a wrench?"

Unable to think of an answer, Nate plopped down on a bench facing the entrance to Sears. I sat down next to him. A row of faceless mannequins, dressed in Fair Isle sweaters and corduroy pants, stared blankly back at us.

"So," I said. "What do you get the people who literally have *everything*?"

Nate laughed. "Literally everything. In piles. All over the house." His laughter quickly turned to a groan, and he put his head in his hands. "It's just like the TV show. Only, there's no hoarding specialist knocking on the door to save the day, and there's no junk guy showing up with a dumpster and a shovel. It's just me, Caity. And I don't know how much more of it I can take."

"Hey." I nudged his shoulder. "It's going to be okay! It's not *that* bad. At least Mom's not storing dead cats in the refrigerator. Right?" I said a silent prayer that Pickles had, in fact, been cremated. "And there's no garbage in the bathtub or rats in the furniture. That's a plus. They're collectors, Nate. That's all. It's their livelihood. They've just gotten carried away and need some help getting back on track. We've already fixed up your room, like I promised, and I'm still working on the rest of the house. We'll get it cleaned up, I promise you. I've got nothing else to do until Christmas."

He raised his head and looked at me, a few wayward chunks of hair sticking out on the sides. He was frecklier than I remembered.

"Exactly," he said. "*Until Christmas*. As soon as you go back to Boston, the mess will pile back up again. Not that I can blame you for taking off. Another year and a half, and I'm out of here, too."

"What do you mean?" I asked, alarmed. "Where are you applying to college?"

He shrugged. "University of California. University of Miami. Penn State. Summers abroad, internships out of state. I learned from the best how to go away and stay away."

My heart sank. Poor Mom and Dad. They were going to be all alone here in Tennessee. It was different when *I* had left—they still had Nate to raise and worry about. But if Nate left, they'd have nobody but each other and a house full of dusty antiques. With nobody around to help, the hoarding probably *would* get worse.

"You don't need to run away," I said, shaking my head. "I know it sounds exciting, and that I'm the last person who should be telling you this because yes, I know, I did it myself, but running away can be very, very lonely. And even if you do make a million friends and you don't miss your family at all, well, they're still going to miss *you*."

"So, what? You want me to go to UT and live at home?"

"No, not at all. You should go to school wherever you want to go to school. That's not my point. My point is...just...don't avoid coming home, Nate. Mom and Dad don't deserve that. *You* didn't deserve that, and I'm sorry."

Nate jammed his hands into his coat pockets, looking extremely uncomfortable. He shared Dad's distaste for discussing emotions, but I didn't care. He deserved the apology.

"So... what are you saying?" he asked. "Are you going to start being around more?"

I shrugged. "I want to try to be. My life is still in Boston, but once I find another job, I can afford to fly back more often to visit. I can spend the holidays here again. It would be sad if every time I came home, you weren't there."

Nate put one foot across his knee and jiggled it up and down. "Why don't you just move back here and marry Mr. M?"

"Excuse me?"

"Come on, I walked in on you guys the other morning."

"We weren't even doing anything! He was tuning my piano."

Nate snorted. "Is that what the old people call it?"

I laughed and whacked him on the arm. "First of all, I'm just older, not *old*. Second of all, Shane.... *Mr. Mitchell*...and I used to be friends. We lost touch, and now"—I waved my hand in the air — "we're catching up. That's it."

"He has a picture of you in his office."

"*What?*"

"Yeah. In his desk drawer. I was going through it looking for a...um...paperclip"—Nate cleared his throat— "and there it was. It looked like it was from band camp or something. You were sitting on the grass wearing this huge, lame T-shirt, and you had your flute in your lap. Mr. M was behind you with his drumsticks, pretending to drum on your head."

"That sounds terrible."

"It's a pretty bad picture. Even so, he doesn't have a bad picture of any other girls in his desk."

I opened my mouth and then snapped it shut again. Thoughts swirled around my head, none of which I wanted to discuss with my little brother.

"Let me get this straight," I said. "Did you say that you were still wearing diapers when you were *eight?*"

Nate laughed and stood up from the bench. "Come on. Let's get this shopping trip over with before Sears runs out of sweatshirts and tools."

"No danger of that," I said, following him past the mannequins, and in the direction of women's clothing.

After we'd picked out a hooded sweatshirt and a chenille bathrobe for Mom, we spent fifteen minutes trying on and modeling ugly Christmas sweaters. The Tran-Siberian Orchestra wailed over the loudspeakers, like we were in some sort of eighties movie montage.

We were in good spirits by the time we made it to the tool department to shop for Dad. It felt good to be back home in Tennessee, Christmas shopping and goofing around with my little brother. Sure, he probably viewed me more as an elderly aunt whom he only saw at weddings and funerals, rather than an older sister to whom he could turn to for advice. But I was going to work on that. I had quite a few things to work on this month. I just had to add it to my list.

CHAPTER 15

I hadn't been joking when I promised Nate that I would continue getting the house in order. As soon as we returned home from Christmas shopping, I called and scheduled a junk removal truck, just like on TV. It was Saturday morning and the truck was now parked in the driveway, and would remain there until seven o'clock tonight. Also remaining until seven o'clock tonight was Shane, whom I'd called and informed that if I was going to dress up as Mrs. Claus in order to help him with *his* project, then he was going to dress up in a pair of coveralls and help me with *my* project. Actually, I'd called and politely asked if he would please help me. He'd agreed, and the five of us now stood in a semicircle on the front lawn, while I attempted to give everybody a pep talk.

"Mom, Dad," I said, using my best hoarding therapist voice. "We want to make this a safe, comfortable environment again. Not just for Nate, but for you guys as well. And for me. I want a home that I can come back to for the holidays without needing to shovel my way into bed. And Mom"—I turned to look her in the eye— "I've been home for a week and I still haven't had that home-cooked meal you promised."

"We've all just been so busy," she said.

"That's not the reason and you know it," I said, trying out a bit of tough love. "The reason is because the stove is covered in naked cherub statues, correct?"

Mom hung her head. "Yes."

"Do naked cherub statues belong on the stove?"

Did naked cherub statues belong anywhere? That was the real question. But I was trying my best to stick to the point.

Mom sighed. "No."

"Good. We're making progress. Now, I understand that it's going to be hard for you guys to let some of this stuff go, but we're all here to support you." I stepped forward and sympathetically squeezed Mom and Dad's shoulders. They looked at each other and shrugged.

Then I turned and looked sternly at Nate and Shane. "Nothing leaves this house without their approval first, okay?" They looked at me and shrugged.

So, we hadn't quite reached the same level of enthusiasm as they do on the television show. It was probably my fault for not inviting over a gaggle of aunts and uncles who could argue and sob and tell tragic stories about Mom and Dad's messed up childhoods. But I did the best that I could on short notice. And, as far as I knew, Mom and Dad's childhoods were both pretty standard. They just really liked antiques.

"Let's do this!" I clapped my hands together and headed for the front porch. I propped open the front door and told Nate and Shane to start hauling stuff onto the lawn, where I'd spread out a bunch of blankets to lay everything on. I got Mom and Dad to agree to a basic plan—anything that couldn't fit either in the back room of the antique shop, the attic, or the barn needed to be junked or donated to charity. The basement of the house was, from now on, reserved for the storage of personal family items only. Once we had a good number of things spread out on the blankets, I started helping Mom and Dad with the process of sorting.

"Diving helmet?" I asked.

"Barn."

"Antique radio with knobs missing and wires hanging out the back?"

Mom wrung her hands and looked at Dad.

"Storage room," said Dad. "I can repair it."

"But you have twenty others that don't need repairing." I motioned toward the blanket behind me filled with antique radios.

"Oh, right," said Dad. "Okay. Donate."

"Junk. Next. Pots and pans that should never touch food again?"

"In the barn with the rest of them."

"Mom."

"They're *supposed* to be green, Caity. It gives them their charm."

"They're corroded."

"They just need cleaning," said Dad. "Then I'm going to re-tin them. Saw it on YouTube."

"Fine," I groaned, moving the pots and pans to the *Barn* blanket. I had to remind myself that antiques were, in fact, how my parents made their living. As long as items were leaving the house and being stored elsewhere, I shouldn't be too hard on them. Getting the house cleared out was the important part. If the barn decided to collapse one day, so be it. Unless, of course, Mom and Dad were *in* the barn when it collapsed. Or burst into flames. Oh, boy. I hadn't even thought of that.

I helped Mom and Dad sort for over an hour before asking Nate to take my place so that Shane and I could start moving items into the barn. Now that thoughts of collapse and fire were in my head, I needed to make sure there was nothing overtly dangerous happening back there. Not that I was a certified barn inspector or anything, but if I noticed the roof was caving in, or there were exposed wires with sparks spraying out of them, I would have to alert the authorities.

I whistled when we walked through the door. The barn wasn't as full as I was expecting—my theory that Mom and Dad had just become a bit lazy in their old age, and started storing things in the house rather than bringing them out here, seemed accurate—but it was still an impressive sight. As I stood looking up at the wide variety of items, I admitted to myself that I was my parents' daughter. Sure, I had rolled my eyes and convinced them to throw away a broken radio, but I still understood that the past was truly fascinating. To let these items become trash—pieces of history that could never be replaced—was unthinkable. I understood why Mom and Dad did what they did, and why they had such a passion for antiques.

I had it too.

I felt suddenly sad that I was going to be leaving in a few weeks. There was so much potential here. If I had the time, I could help them so much more. I could set up a better system and help them to expand the business. Mom and Dad had sometimes talked about selling things on eBay, but they'd never managed to find the time. I felt a flutter of excitement as I thought about researching each of the items stacked up in the barn, putting them up for sale on eBay, and sending them off to new homes around the world to be treasured and enjoyed.

I'd enjoyed my time working for a publisher of history books. But in the end, books were just books. What was piled up in front of me in the barn were bits and pieces of real, tangible history—actual things that people had used every day in their homes. I walked over and pushed down the lever on a vintage toaster. A Sunbeam T-9, which was state-of-the art during its time. I thought about my high school computer monitor, also state-of-the art during its time, now abandoned on the front porch. Everything changed so quickly these days. Without people like

Mom and Dad, these pieces of history would be lost forever. As much as I wanted to get back to the cleanup project, I was also dying to start digging around in the barn.

"What are you smiling about?" asked Shane, setting the box he'd been carrying on a table and joining me by the toaster.

"Just thinking," I said. "Some of this stuff is so cool. It's been a long time since I really looked at any of it, you know?"

"You ever think about taking over the store...after your parents retire?"

"I don't think people actually retire from owning antique shops, do they?"

Shane laughed. "Hypothetically, let's say that someday they retire."

I brushed the dust off a rocking chair before sinking down into it. "I honestly never thought about it. I mean, I'm only twenty-six, and Mom and Dad are relatively young. I've been enjoying being away, doing my own thing." I shrugged. "I really haven't thought about it."

"But now you're unemployed."

"Yes, thank you for reminding me. What's your point?"

"My point is that things are different now," said Shane, sitting in the matching rocker next to mine, like two old folks at the nursing home. "You have options. What do you have that's tying you to Boston?"

I frantically searched my mind for an answer. Job? No. Boyfriend? Nope. Handful of casual acquaintances that I would never miss? Sure thing. But I couldn't tell that to Shane. It was true there wasn't much tying me to Boston, but coming back permanently to Reindeer Falls? It felt too much like giving up. Too pathetic.

"There are so many publishers and museums in the Northeast," I said. "You said it yourself, I have options now. I could look for a job in New York if I wanted. If I come back to Tennessee, all those options go away."

"True," said Shane, "but you do have a family business here in Tennessee. Last time I checked, you weren't the heir to the Metropolitan Museum of Art."

I rubbed the bridge of my nose. "I know, but...moving back *home?*" I groaned and slumped down in the rocker. "After going to *Harvard?*"

"So, what? You think you're better than everyone else who lives in this town just because you went to Harvard?"

I sat up straighter. "No, of course not. I just meant—"

"Do you remember Brent Donovan? From high school?" interrupted Shane.

"Yeah."

"Well, he went away to college and now he's back in town running his grandmother's knitting shop."

"Get out."

"I'm serious. No matter where you went to school, there's no shame in coming home, Caitlin. Home is home. It's actually pretty nice here."

"First of all, you sound like a poorly written tourism pamphlet. Second of all, I never said that I was better than anybody else, or that I was *ashamed* to come home."

"But that was partly why you left, wasn't it?"

I stared at him, my eyes narrowed. "How do you even know these things about me?"

He stared back at me, his eyes searching my face. "What'd you do, forget everything we talked about that night? You told me more about yourself than I'd learned in four years of knowing you. Always the quiet one, except for that one night before you left for college."

Ah, that was right. The night before I left.

Ice cream at Swirls & Scoops, followed by a walk around town and talking. I remembered being so incredibly comfortable with this person I was going to have to leave behind very shortly. I remembered spilling my guts because I knew we were very likely to never see each other again. Little had I known that a celestial clock was ticking, counting down the minutes until Shane would tell me that he loved me and everything would go haywire. On the other hand, maybe I had known exactly what was coming. Maybe I had sensed a sort of electricity in the air between us, and I'd finally opened up so that when he told me how he felt, it wouldn't land with such a thud. And it had worked, somewhat.

It had just been too late.

"Okay, fine," I said, rocking gently in the chair. "I did leave partly because I was stressed out, and ashamed, and I didn't want to deal with my parents' mess. But I also left because I worked hard and I got a scholarship, and because you don't give up the chance to go to Harvard. And just so you know, I'm not ashamed of my family anymore. What I'm ashamed of is that I never came back to help them."

"You're here now," said Shane. "Which makes me happier than you know." He reached over and put his hand on top of mine, resting on the arm of the rocker. Two old folks at the home, a lifetime of shared memories between them. Or, four years of high school and an ice cream cone. I turned my hand over, interlacing our fingers, and I smiled.

"It's almost like we're back on that band bus," I said. "Sitting here, side-by-side."

"We never held hands on the bus," he pointed out.

"No."

"I wouldn't have minded."

"Yeah?"

"Yeah."

We sat in silence for a few seconds. It was chilly in the barn, but the back of my neck felt warm, and the minimal bit of contact between our hands was sending shivers through my body. I leaned my head against the back of the rocker and turned to look at him.

"I did come back that first Christmas," I said. It was time that he knew.

He leaned his head back also, and turned to face me. His eyes questioning. "I assumed you had come back for Christmas break. But I never saw you."

I nodded. "I was going to tell you I had changed my mind. That I wanted to be with you." My voice cracked a bit and my chest tightened. I never thought I'd be telling this to Shane. I'd thought this chapter of my life was over. But maybe this was a good thing, getting it all out, letting him know after all this time. Was this what they called closure? I supposed if I was leaving again in a few weeks, then it had to be.

"But then I was at the diner for lunch, on my first day back, and your mom came in. She was chatting with Tammy, and I overheard her say that you were seeing a girl you'd met at school. Your mom said that she was coming to your house for Christmas. So"—I shrugged and bit my lip— "I couldn't go through with it. You'd moved on. I was too late."

Shane ran his hand through his hair and let out a sigh. "That must've been Amy. We broke up about three weeks after Christmas." He looked at me, his eyes darkening. "I would've ended it sooner, Caity, if I'd known. I would've done *anything*, if I'd known. You should have told me."

He lifted my hand and brought it to his lips, kissing it gently. Had I not been fully shrouded by a dusty, hooded sweatshirt, I could almost imagine him continuing up my arm, all the way to my neck. I shuddered and stood up, pulling him to standing in front of me. Aware that my parents or Nate could walk in at any moment, I led him to the back of the barn and behind a barricade of antique dressers. I put my arms around his neck.

So, this didn't feel quite like closure.

"How come you never tried to reach me?" I asked, looking up at him. "When I didn't call you from Boston...how come you

113

didn't try to call, or email, or hop a plane to make some grand romantic gesture?"

"Because I'd wanted you to know how I felt, but I was never planning to pursue it," he said, putting his hands on my lower back. "Because I always knew that you were too smart and too good for me. Because I never for a minute thought that you felt the same way."

He trailed off as I grabbed a fistful of hair and pulled him toward me and into a kiss. His body felt solid beneath the softness of his sweatshirt. I ran my hands down to the top of his jeans, hooking my fingers over the waistband. He laughed lightly against my mouth and opened his eyes.

"Caity."

"What?"

"Not here."

"Okay, let's go to your house."

He pried both my hands out of his jeans and walked me a few steps back until we were leaning against the barn wall. There were probably a billion spiders behind me, but at the moment I didn't care. I could shower later. Shane, too. Wow, wrong thought. Every single nerve ending in my body was suddenly turned up to full blast. I ran my hands down and under his sweatshirt, under his T-shirt, and over his stomach. That was no doughy band director body under there. Maybe I was wrong when I'd told Emma that he was no Tom Brady.

With a groan, Shane took half a step back, my hands dropping out from the bottom of his sweatshirt. "We have to stop."

"No, we don't," I said, grabbing the cords on his sweatshirt and playfully pulling him toward me. He lost his resolve for a few more delightful seconds, until finally I was the one who let him go. "I suppose we haven't even had a first date yet, huh?"

"That's what I've been trying to say, you nympho."

I laughed. "Don't act so surprised. Everybody's always so surprised. Yes, I'm quiet and I read a lot of books. Why does everyone assume that makes me some kind of a nun?" I walked around behind Shane and smacked him on the butt. "I'm no nun."

He turned partway around, a look of shock on his face, cheeks red. It wasn't the first time I'd made Shane Mitchell blush.

"It was never that I didn't want you," I said, turning serious. "And I was never too smart or too good for you. We were just so young...and we ran out of time."

"Well, we're older now," said Shane, giving me a look that sent shivers down my spine. "And if you decide to stay, we could have all the time in the world."

CHAPTER 16

"We're going to need another extension cord," I shouted to Shane, wherever he was. The two cords already connected to the hot chocolate machine still weren't going to reach the outlet in the garage.

It was five thirty on Sunday afternoon, and I was decked out in full Mrs. Claus attire—horrid green velvet dress, wire-rimmed eyeglasses, curly white wig. A moment later, Shane came out of the garage dragging a heavy-duty extension cord and wearing his rented Santa suit. Earlier in the evening I'd helped him put on his beard, and stuffed a pillow into his stomach area, which was, oddly enough, a bit of a turn-on.

"Let there be cocoa!" he declared as the machine sprang to life. "Ho! Ho! Ho!"

We'd set up a long metal table with the hot chocolate machine and an assortment of baked goods. My mother, thrilled to be able to use her oven again (the naked cherub statues having been relocated to the barn), had baked us several batches of brownies. A jar sat on the corner of the table with a sign, *Donations to Save the Reindeer Falls Community Center*, taped to the front. Officer

Hutchinson had even volunteered to come by to help with traffic control, which I thought was sweet, but probably unnecessary.

"If anyone recognizes me, you're both dead," said Nate, who was stuffed inside a reindeer costume.

"Oh, buck up," I said, laughing at my own joke. Nate just rolled his eyes and wandered off. He would never have agreed to dress up as Clip-Clop if it had been me who'd asked him. But it had been Shane who'd asked, and Nate had agreed as a favor to his favorite teacher.

At five minutes to six, Shane went inside the house, flicked on the lights, and turned on the sound system.

JOOOOY TOOOOOO THE WORLD!!!!!!!!

Music blasting, we waited side-by-side on the lawn, like king and queen of the North Pole. At precisely five minutes past six, the cars started pouring in. I recognized so many people that I'd gone to high school with, quite a few of them arriving with their husbands, wives, and young children. There was also the entire Clemson family, Tammy Pulaski and her husband, and Dottie Cross—wrapped in a white fur coat like a little polar bear. Even Miss Annabeth turned up with Giles Wilson.

"Thank you so much for doing this," she said to Shane, patting him on the cheek. "You're a dear."

"That would be Nate," he said, pointing to my brother, whose antlers had gone a bit lopsided. Shane gave me a wink. "But, you're very welcome, Miss Annabeth."

As more people arrived, they kept staring and doing double takes, trying to figure out who it was Shane had roped into playing Mrs. Claus. When they realized it was me—that I was back in Reindeer Falls, and that I was being an active participant in the community after all this time—I was greeted with hugs, smiles, and warmth.

"IS THIS YOUR HOUSE?" yelled Dottie Cross, who was both senile and hard of hearing. "IS THAT YOUR HUSBAND?"

"Of course!" I said, embracing my role. "Santa and I have been married for a hundred years!"

"NOT SANTA, YOU FOOL!" she yelled. "SHANE MITCHELL! THE MUSIC TEACHER! ARE YOU MARRIED TO HIM?"

So, not quite as senile as I'd imagined. I cleared my throat and glanced at Shane, who was laughing at me from behind his beard. "No, Ms. Cross. We're not *really* married. I'm just helping out an old friend."

Dottie squeezed my arm with a surprisingly firm grip. She looked sternly into my eyes, as if she was about to scold me, or perhaps send me to the principal's office, then shook her head and shuffled off back to her car.

"Should she be driving at night?" I asked, rubbing my arm, as Shane came up beside me. The car door slammed and the engine roared to life, blinding us with headlights.

"Probably not."

I held my breath as Dottie pulled slowly away from the curb and was waved along by Officer Hutchinson. We watched as the taillights of her car disappeared slowly down the road.

"Santa!" Several children ran over to greet us and Shane quickly got back into character, putting his arm around my shoulders. I slipped an arm around his waist.

"Hello, children!" I said, hoping that I sounded like a hospitable old woman, rather than the witch from Hansel and Gretel. "Have you told Santa what you want for Christmas?"

Shane bent down and patiently listened while each child told him what they wanted. Video game systems I'd never even heard of. Pokémon cards. One kid wanted his own iPhone. I smiled when I thought of the things I used to get for Christmas. Books. A carte-de-visite photograph of Abraham Lincoln. One year, Dad refinished this gorgeous antique vanity table for my bedroom. It was covered in ornate carvings and had a padded stool. I'd felt like a princess.

"Ho! Ho! Ho!" laughed Shane. "Looks like Santa's going to need to make a visit to the Apple store!"

"And Amazon!" added one of the kids.

The parents all laughed, and as I took their children off to find some cookies and torment my brother, I heard them complimenting Shane on the high school band's holiday concert. A real pillar of the community he'd become. I smiled and shook my head.

Around seven o'clock, a reporter from the *Reindeer Falls Gazette* showed up and took a photo of Shane, me, and Clip-Clop in front of the house. Mom, who had stopped by to help man the snack table, gazed at the two of us with huge, hopeful mother-of-the-bride eyes.

Michelle and Emma came by right after the photo shoot, and we had a big group hug, as it was the first time the three of us had been together in a very long time.

"Santa and Mrs. Claus," said Emma, shaking her head at me. "I told you. Didn't I tell you?"

"I thought you said you weren't doing any man hunting?" asked Michelle, raising an eyebrow.

"Do I look like I'm man hunting right now?" I asked, motioning to the absurd outfit I was wearing.

"I know one man who'd be into that look," said Emma, and the two of them looked across the yard at Santa.

"Okay," I said. "It's been a lovely reunion with the two of you. Now you may leave." Laughing, I pushed them both in the direction of the refreshments.

By the time eight o'clock rolled around, the donation jar was full, and all the refreshments were gone. Almost everybody had left, and we said thank you and goodnight to Officer Hutchinson. She was planning to stop by Dottie Cross's house to make sure she had made it home safely, which was the type of thing I missed about living in a small town. Actually, this whole evening was the type of thing I missed about living in a small town. Once everybody had gone, Shane and I stood alone again, side-by-side, on the front lawn.

"I would call that a success," said Shane. "The kids had fun. The donation jar is full. There's going to be an embarrassing photo of Nate in tomorrow's newspaper."

"Clearly, the best part," I said, giving Shane a high-five.

Then, as "Frosty the Snowman" came on for the hundredth time that night, I pulled his beard down beneath his chin, and kissed him.

"You were sweet to do this for Miss Annabeth," I said. "Thank you."

"You're very welcome." He wrapped his arms around my waist and pulled me closer.

"Your belly pillow's in the way," I mumbled, resting my head on his chest.

"Maybe you should take it out," he mumbled back.

I laughed and gently punched his middle. "Maybe after dinner. I don't know about you, but I'm starved."

I took a step back, pulled off my wig and shook out my hair. Then, with a wink, I headed into the house to change.

* * *

I FLICKED through the photos on Shane's phone, smiling and shaking my head. "They're really living it up down there. What's the name of where they live again?"

"Sunset Havens," said Shane. "The second-largest retirement community in Florida. They get everywhere by golf cart and they play pool volleyball."

"Sunset Havens," I repeated. "Good for them. Your parents have seen some serious stuff during their careers. Let them look at palm trees and golf courses for the rest of their lives. Who's this guy?" I pointed at a picture of Shane's mom with a guy about our age. He was wearing a neon orange polo shirt.

"That's my mom's friend's son," said Shane. "Graham Blenderman. He's down there all the time. The old ladies love him."

"He looks...interesting." I pushed the phone back across the table.

We had just finished dinner and were drinking the last of our wine. Half a bottle of merlot, and the sight of Shane sitting across the table was starting to wear me down. Black button-up shirt with the sleeves rolled to the elbows, his drummer's forearms on display. A dreamy filter of candlelight between us.

"Do you remember the first time we talked...freshman year?" he asked, leaning closer across the table. The candle flickered and trace notes of leather and cedar drifted toward me. I leaned in closer, trying to breathe him in without being too obvious. "It's okay," he whispered. "You smell good, too." I smiled and gently tapped his foot under the table.

"Of course, I remember," I said. "It was on the bus. We were on our way to a football game against the Highlanders. You asked me why I was so quiet, and I hated you for it."

His eyebrows drew together. "I thought you were cute."

"Then you should have put a little effort into coming up with a better line," I said.

"Hey, I planned my attack for ten whole minutes. The point of which was to get your attention. Love me or hate me, it put me on your radar."

"That it did," I said, taking another sip of wine.

"So, which was it?"

"Huh?"

"In the end. Did you love me or hate me?"

I studied his face across the table, blue eyes sparkling with mischief, but also a flicker of something else. A flicker of our shared history. Memories of all the laughs, the questions, the teasing. The random times we had been there to comfort each other, when nobody else would have sufficed. But there were some moments we didn't share—memories that were mine alone.

The crush I'd had on him. The girlfriends who were never me. The agony of leaving for college the morning after our first kiss, and the years I'd spent wondering about what could have been.

"I loved you," I admitted, nodding as my eyes misted over. "The best part of my day was when you swaggered up the aisle of that bus, like you were some sort of hot ticket, and you flopped down next to *me*. I never understood why you did it, either. But I was always glad that you did." I paused to take a deep breath. "So yeah, I loved you, Shane. And I've spent eight years wondering what it could have been like if we'd only had more time."

"Then don't go back to Boston," he said, his eyes pleading with me. "Last time, you left because you had no choice. But this time, you do. You could go back long enough to pack up your things, and then you could come back to me."

You could come back to me. The words sent an ache of longing deep into my chest.

"I can't decide that right now," I said, leaning back. "I have, you know, a *life* out there. I have friends, and... and..." I trailed off. Why did it seem like I was always trying to convince people that I had a life? I couldn't possibly have lived somewhere for eight years and not have anything to show for it, could I? The thought was too depressing to bear.

"I know," said Shane. "It's a lot to ask. I understand."

"It's a really big decision," I said. "A hard decision."

But looking at him across the table, the idea of leaving him behind slicing my heart into two, I knew it wasn't nearly as hard of a decision as I thought.

"So, I was checking out the baby grand in your living room, earlier," I said, changing the subject, but not taking my eyes off of his. "While you were getting changed for dinner."

"Oh, yeah?"

"Yeah." My eyes flicked down to the billfold on the table, and then back up at Shane. The check had been paid. We were free to go.

"And?"

"And I was thinking that maybe I'd like to try it out."

Twenty minutes later, pushing through the front door of Shane's house, I caught a glimpse of the baby grand in the living room. I did want to play it, that hadn't just been a line. Only...later.

"Longest...car ride...ever," I said as we tripped, laughing, up the stairs. Torture was more like it. We passed Mr. Mitchell's study on the right, the infamous bathroom on the left, and then I stopped short in the middle of the hallway. "Where do you sleep?" It struck me as quite funny that Shane might own this big house and still sleep in his high school bedroom.

"I've redecorated the master," he said, pulling me into a bedroom a bit further down the hall. There were no traces of Mr. and Mrs. Mitchell to be seen. Just light gray walls, dark wood furniture, and a king-sized bed.

"Thank God," I said, and I kicked the door shut.

* * *

I ROLLED over the next morning and screamed.

Instead of finding Shane's warm body beside me, I found Mr. Mitchell's model skeleton stretched out on top of the covers, dressed in nothing but a pair of boxer shorts. A note was attached to one of its ribs with a twisty tie.

Caity –

I always knew you'd be the death of me.

- Shane

P.S. Not actually dead. Making coffee. See you soon.

CHAPTER 17

"*Y*ou know you've been *glowing* this entire morning?" asked Emma, tossing her long, blonde hair over her shoulder and glancing at me. She was giving me a ride home from our rehearsal at the community center. We could have rehearsed at my house, but I wanted to practice a bit on the piano I'd be playing at the show.

"Well, it's been a pretty great week," I admitted, looking out the window. Shane and I had been practically inseparable ever since our date. He'd been giving me piano lessons on his baby grand, and despite the many breaks we ended up taking, I was quickly becoming comfortable with playing again. "Shane and I"—I shook my head. "Who knew?"

"*I* knew, dummy," said Emma. "So, can I get the juicy details or what?"

"What kind of a girl do you think I am?" I asked, placing one hand on my chest. "I mean, I don't even know what to *call* half of the things we've done."

The car swerved as Emma burst out laughing. She steadied the wheel and gave me a stern look. "You know you shouldn't say those things while I'm driving."

"Sorry." I smiled. "I'm home, anyway. I'll have to tell you another time."

"The house looks good, by the way." She leaned down and looked through the passenger window. "I drove by once—right after I'd come back to Reindeer Falls—and there was stuff all over the front porch. I swear I saw a computer monitor."

I snorted. "We've been making progress. I just hope it stays that way after I leave."

"You're still planning on leaving, huh?"

I shrugged. "I *have* to, Em. I've lived in Boston for eight years. I can't just be expected to drop everything and move back home."

"And what about this great thing you've got happening with Shane?"

I shrugged again, not wanting to think about it. "We'll figure something out."

Emma responded with a stern look that reminded me quite a bit of the one I got from Dottie Cross. I wrapped my arms protectively around my chest.

"You're not going to pinch me, are you?" I asked.

"Huh?"

"Never mind."

Emma sighed and changed the subject, motioning toward the house. "Just don't throw away anything valuable. I heard that pogs are worth, like, millions now."

"Duly noted," I said, getting out of the car. "See you later."

"Later."

I walked into the quiet house and grabbed a bottle of water out of the refrigerator, admiring how scrubbed and organized the kitchen looked. So far, so good. It being a Thursday morning, Mom and Dad were at the antique shop and Nate was at school. Shane was also at school, which was too bad since I was dying to see him. Like a drug-sniffing dog, I made my way to my bedroom where a sweater he'd forgotten was draped across the back of a chair. I picked it up and buried my nose in it. Sinking down into

125

the chair, I hugged the sweater to my chest. I stared at the box on the floor that I had started filling with items I planned to take back with me to Boston. My plan was to get rid of everything in this room that didn't fit into that box. Could I fit a twenty-six-year-old man in there too? I'd probably have to take out a few things.

My throat tightened. It had been less than twenty-four hours since I'd last seen Shane, and I was already desperate to see him again. How did I expect to be able to go back to Massachusetts? Even if we agreed to attempt a long-distance relationship, I couldn't live with this feeling all the time. I couldn't walk around the streets of Boston with a sweater strapped beneath my nose like a feed bag. Never mind that Shane was constantly busy on the weekends with band practices and putting up lavish displays of Christmas lights. What had I gotten myself into?

I walked over to the closet. It was the last part of my room that needed to be cleaned. The floor and upper shelf were piled high with boxes and plastic bags. Half of my high school wardrobe still hung from the wooden bar. With a trash bag to my left, and the box to my right, I started the process. I had forged my way into the very back of the closet, when I found two large trash bags with masking tape stuck to them. *BB's,* they said. BB's? Curiously, I pulled one bag to the front of the closet—it was both soft and heavy—and untied the top.

Beanie Babies. Loads of them.

I started to laugh. Somehow, until I found myself staring into that trash bag, I had completely forgotten about the fact that I was a one-time collector of Beanie Babies. And not just any Beanie Babies. Oh, no. I'd waited in lines for limited editions, I'd gone to flea markets with my parents, and my nine-year-old self had haggled with dealers over ones that I knew were rare. I was hardcore before I was even ten.

"Holy cow," I murmured as I started pulling them out, one by one. They were all in mint condition and still had all their tags. I dragged the bag over to my computer, opened up eBay, and started typing in names. Nuts the squirrel—four dollars. Pinchers the lobster—one dollar. Princess Diana commemorative purple bear—four thousand dollars.

I froze and placed one hand over my mouth. Four *thousand* dollars? That must be a mistake. I tried to remain calm and pulled out a few more.

Gobbles the turkey—six dollars. Iggy the iguana—three dollars. Valentina with tag errors—twelve thousand dollars.

Twelve thousand dollars? I checked the tag. Tag errors were a funny thing—a simple misspelling, or a missing space between words, could launch the value of an item through the roof. Sure enough, my Valentina had the error on the tag. I plugged a few more names into eBay before letting out a whoop and jumping up and down on my bed.

Feeling slightly dizzy, I climbed down from the bed and lay down on the floor, staring up at the ceiling. All this time, I'd been sitting on a fuzzy, pellet-filled gold mine. I had thousands of dollars' worth of Beanie Babies in those bags. I could almost single-handedly save the community center! This was incredible news, but the thought of returning to Boston still hung over me, clouding my excitement.

Being with Shane was what I wanted. Clearly. Being back in Reindeer Falls, close to my family, and waking up to Shane every morning, wouldn't exactly be a tragic ending to this story. On the other hand, I had a degree from Harvard. Not that I thought that fact made me better than anybody else, as Shane had suggested. That wasn't it. It was just that such a prestigious degree came with a lot of opportunities. I had stayed in my textbook publishing job for so long because it was comfortable and because it was a steady source of income. But maybe being laid off was a blessing. Maybe I was being given the opportunity to finally find something really great. There had to be a reason I'd spent nearly a decade living on the East Coast, right? Something great could be just over the horizon. If I gave up now, I'd never know.

Not that being with Shane and my family would be *giving up*, exactly. Saying that sounded wrong and left me with a sad feeling. It's just that, I would miss Boston if I left. I had my routines. I had my daily stop at Starbucks on the way to the T station every morning. Of course, Starbucks didn't have the same charm of Holly's, but what did? There was also the organic grocery store down the street where Ben and I used to do our shopping every Thursday night. They had free wine and cheese samples after five o'clock.

Free cheese?

Was that what I was going back for? Of course not. There was also my hairdresser on Newbury Street. Not that I could afford to get my hair done on Newbury Street anymore. And there were all those malls that I didn't need to drive an hour to get to. Although, that trip to the mall with Nate had actually been pretty fun. But there was no need to make a regular thing out of it. I mean, Nate was family, and family was...

Expendable? Something to be taken for granted? Visited only when it was convenient?

I closed my eyes, willing the voice that kept piping up in my head to please shut it. Of course, that wasn't how I felt about my family. I wasn't being fair to myself. It'd be one thing if I had nothing back in Boston. If I'd been some kind of loser who'd spent eight years in a place and hadn't put down a single root, then it would make sense to move back to Reindeer Falls. But that wasn't me. Was it? One stubborn thought kept pushing its way to the surface. A thought that said everything I had listed as a reason to stay in Boston was completely superficial.

The sound of my ringing cell phone pulled me out of my own head, and back into my bedroom. I sat up, grabbed my phone off the desk, and read the name on the screen.

Ben.

Great. What did *he* want? I hadn't spoken to him in weeks. Not since I'd thrown him out of our apartment. He'd texted me shortly after—when I was already back in Reindeer Falls—asking if it was okay for him to come by the apartment to get the rest of his things. I'd told him that I was out of town, and he was welcome to come by. I'd hoped that was the end of it. What could he possibly want now? We didn't share any pets or bank accounts. It was a clean and easy split. With a slight hesitation, I answered the phone.

"Hello?"

"Caitlin. Hey. How've you been?"

"I'm fine, Ben," I said, my jaw clenching at the sound of his cheating voice. "Can I help you with something?"

"Oh. Um, yeah." He sounded thrown by my briskness. Good. "It's just that when I came by the other day to get the rest of my stuff, I noticed your closet looked sort of ransacked. Like you'd left in a hurry. I was just wondering...not that it's any of my business, but.... where'd you go?"

"It's *not* any of your business," I said. "But I'm back in Tennessee. Family emergency."

"Everything okay?"

"Not really. That's why I said family emergency instead of family fun time."

"Caity, I was just—"

"You don't need to worry about me or my family, Ben," I said, getting irritated. "Thanks to that little love note of yours, we're not together anymore. Remember?"

"Caity, I'm—"

"Save it. Was there another reason you called?"

"There was, yeah." He cleared his throat. "I heard from Mike that you'd lost your job."

Mike was a mutual friend of ours, and a coworker of mine. He'd gotten the axe too.

"That's correct."

129

"I'm sorry, Caity. Between that, and us, and now this family emergency, I feel really bad."

"I don't need your pity."

"It's not pity, Caity. It's just me, wanting to help."

"I don't need your pity *or* your help."

"Just listen. Please."

I picked up a Beanie Baby, squeezing its neck between my hands.

"My dad knows a guy at Houghton Mifflin," he continued. "My dad really liked you, and he's pretty mad at me for...for what happened. He said if you want a job over there, all he has to do is make a few calls. You'd need to come in for an interview, but only as a technicality."

I released my grip on the Beanie Baby. "A job?"

"Yeah."

"At Houghton Mifflin?"

Ben chuckled. *"Yeah."*

I dropped Inky the Octopus on the floor and sank down onto my bed. So, it wasn't actually Ben who wanted to help me, it was Ben's father. And Houghton Mifflin was a very big deal. Sure, they were another textbook publisher, which wasn't exactly my life's dream, but they were a huge company. I could donate the Beanie Baby money to the community center and go back to a secure job in Boston. This could be the great thing I'd been waiting for.

"That's very nice of your *father,*" I said. "I just...I'm going to need some time to think about it. Can I let you know? Does this offer have a time limit?"

"Of course not. Take your time. Let me know after the holidays."

"Okay. Thanks."

We sat in silence for a few moments.

"I'm really sorry, Caity," he said, at last. "You didn't deserve what I did. I don't expect you to forgive me. But I want you to know that I really am sorry."

I rolled my eyes, certain the only thing Ben was sorry about was that his father was mad at him, and probably withholding cash.

"Have a good Christmas, Ben," I said with a sigh. "I'll be in touch."

"Okay. You too."

"Bye."

I hung up the phone and stared at my box of belongings on the floor. That phone call was so out of left field. So unexpected. I had so many conflicting emotions racing around inside my head, there was only one thing I could think of that might help me calm down and allow me to think. I walked down the hall to the living room and stood in front of the piano. It was funny how I'd survived eight years without it, and now it was the first place I ran to.

There was a book of Christmas songs already up on the stand, from when I'd played for my family the other night. The fireplace —recently inspected and back in commission—had been roaring, and the Christmas tree had been twinkling in the front window. Everything I'd envisioned when I'd first come back to Reindeer Falls had finally become a reality. Shane had even stopped by, and we'd all played a game of Trivial Pursuit. That was the night he'd forgotten his sweater.

I sat down on the bench and flipped through the pages until I found what I was looking for. "Auld Lang Syne." It was more of a New Year's song than a Christmas song, but it had always been my favorite. There was something haunting about the melody that always cut right through me, making me feel emotions that I could never put into words. Every bar of it perfectly matched my mood that afternoon. With my soul pouring into those keys, and a million unmade decisions inside my head, I played.

CHAPTER 18

$\mathcal{A}$s much as I'd wanted to see Shane prior to my phone call from Ben, I spent the rest of the day avoiding him. I walked into town later that afternoon to see if Mom and Dad needed any help at the store. I inhaled deeply as I walked along the country road, enjoying the fresh air and the utter lack of people. The contrast between Reindeer Falls and Boston still astounded me on a daily basis. Walking around Harvard Square was a mass confusion of people crisscrossing on sidewalks and going in every which direction. It was sensory overload of beeping horns, exhaust fumes, and watching where you stepped. I enjoyed it on some level. There was an energy in the city that you didn't get out here in the country. And as an introvert, it was always nice to find myself lost in a crowd, one face among many. I could spend days, if I wanted, not speaking to anybody other than the Starbucks barista.

On the other hand, being an introvert in the city was exhausting. The constant noise and the dodging of people. The jostling and the rude looks on the subway. I'd experienced all aspects of the big city life over the past eight years, and as I walked along the country road, I toyed with the idea that maybe I'd had

132

enough. What would it be like to live here again? How would it feel to wake up each morning and drive to Christmas Past? To get my morning coffee from Holly's and my lunch from The Greasy Antler? What would it be like to have close, meaningful friendships again? Both Emma and Michelle seemed to be considering settling down again in Reindeer Falls.

Once I had graduated from college and moved into the working world, new friendships came to a screeching halt. I wasn't the type to just go out and meet people. Meeting new people and making small talk gave me anxiety. It didn't help that every time I turned on the television, I saw images of single women bonding over shoe shopping and cocktails. I often wondered what was wrong with me. While I'd managed to make a few close friends during my time in college, we'd all gone our separate ways after graduation—something that seemed to be the story of my life.

The idea of having my childhood girlfriends around me again was tempting. Being part of a tight-knit social circle was certainly something I missed. Still, returning to Reindeer Falls and latching onto my childhood friends seemed like the easy way out. Shouldn't I, as a functioning human being, be able to form new friendships? A familiar stab of shame and self-doubt hit me in the stomach.

Over the past week, Shane and I had avoided talking about my leaving, but we couldn't avoid it forever. Now that I needed to give Ben an answer about the job, we were going to have to talk about it very soon. If I decided to go back to Boston for good, he needed to understand that it wasn't because he had done anything wrong. It was simply because I had a life and opportunities to pursue outside of Reindeer Falls.

"Caity!" said Mom, as I pushed through the door of Christmas Past. "Brian, Caity's here!"

"Hello!" shouted Dad, from somewhere out back.

"I came by to see if you needed any help," I said, slinging my purse up onto the counter.

"Did you walk here?" Mom looked concerned. "Your cheeks are all red. You should have called us for a ride!"

"I had some things to think about." I shrugged, wishing that red cheeks were my biggest concern. "I needed the walk."

"Well, we could certainly use your help today, love. Come on back."

Mom looked so genuinely happy to see me, that my eyes brimmed with tears. She led me into the back room and sent Dad up front to man the register. On one of the worktables sat a beautiful, but heavily tarnished, pewter tea set. Next to it sat a sponge and a bowl full of a white paste. I knew that mixture well —salt, vinegar, and flour. When I was younger, Mom and Dad always let me help out with the polishing. I pulled up a stool and happily set to work. Mom pulled up a stool next to me with a bowl and sponge of her own. We worked in silence for a while, with Mom casting me the occasional sidelong glance that she thought I didn't notice. This little polishing task was obviously part of her plan to get me to spill.

"So," she said, holding a polished teacup in the air and checking her work. "What were you, um, thinking about as you walked here?"

"Oh, this and that," I said, dipping my sponge into the paste. "That and this."

"Nothing, um, in particular?"

"Nah." I slowly scrubbed at the spout of the teapot. "Well, I did think about *one* thing."

She perked up. "Oh?"

I put the teapot down and looked her seriously in the eyes. "Netflix or Hulu, Mom? Which one should I go with?"

She slammed her teacup down on the bench and I bit my lip, trying not to laugh.

"I'm sorry," I said. "I'm just kidding. If you must know, I was

134

thinking about whether or not I should move back to Boston. Happy?"

"*Yes*," she said. "You've always been such a clam. It's like pulling teeth getting you to talk."

I smiled. "Be honored, Mom. You're one of very few people I actually do talk to."

"So, tell me," she said, picking up another teacup. "What's making this such a tough decision? You know you'll always have a job here at the shop. More than a job, actually. Your father and I are getting older, Caity, and we've been thinking about how we'd love for you to—"

"Ben called," I interrupted.

"Oh," said Mom. As the news sank in, she began shaking her head fervently back and forth. "Do *not* give that boy another chance, Caity. Once a cheater, always a—"

"It's not like that," I interrupted again. "He just...he feels bad. Or, rather, his father feels bad. Anyway, his father knows a guy over at Houghton Mifflin, and he's offering me a job. If I want it, it's mine."

"And do you want it?" she asked, calming down a bit.

"Of *course*, I want it. I mean, a few weeks ago I didn't know how I was going to pay my rent. I was considering moving back here out of necessity. Now, I have this fantastic opportunity. I'd be crazy to give it up."

"And what about Shane?" asked Mom, softly. "Is he not a necessity?"

I sighed. "We haven't really talked about it yet."

As if on cue, the bells on the front door jingled as a customer came into the shop. A moment later, Dad poked his head into the back room. "Someone here to see you, Caity."

I looked at Mom, my eyebrows raised. She shrugged and turned back to polishing the pewter, her manner suggesting that if I had made my bed, perhaps I should shut up and lie in it. I quickly washed my hands and walked through the door into the front of the shop. As I suspected, Shane was standing at the counter, flipping through a box of antique cabinet photos. He let out a whistle.

"Mr. Cook, what is *this*?" He held up a sepia-toned photo of a burlesque dancer.

Dad's face turned red. "Not sure how that got in there," he said, his head bobbing up and down. "Better go see Sandra about something." He plucked the photo out of Shane's hand and ducked quickly into the back room.

"I've been trying to reach you all afternoon," said Shane, leaning his elbows on the counter, blue eyes looking me over. "Where've you been?"

"Rehearsal. Then I walked here to see if Mom and Dad needed any help."

He narrowed his eyes. "Everything okay?"

I looked over my shoulder to make sure Mom and Dad weren't watching, then I leaned across the counter for a kiss. His skin was cold from outside, and I had the overwhelming desire to warm him up. But there was too much counter between us, and too many parents in the next room. I sighed and ran one hand down his stubbly cheek. "Sort of."

Shane took a step back, his eyebrows furrowed. "What's up?"

"It's a total cliché, but...we need to talk."

"Uh-oh."

"Can we go somewhere?"

"Of course," he said. "Have you been to the Falls since you've been back?"

"Not yet." I shook my head. "Just give me one sec."

"Sure."

I stepped into the back room and apologized to Mom and Dad for only staying long enough to polish one teapot. Dad seemed unoffended, but Mom waved me away, clearly annoyed about more than just the teapot.

Shane and I crossed the town square, passed the community

center, and walked up the path to the Falls hand-in-hand. The sound of rushing water became closer and closer, until there it was in front of us. Measuring in at eighty-four feet high, the Reindeer Falls waterfall was no Niagara. But it was beautiful, and it was a source of pride for our tiny town—whether or not a reindeer had ever actually appeared from within its mist. It was also a source of secluded benches upon which to make-out with your high school boyfriend. I'd been here a few times with Colin, back in the day, and I was sure he'd kept up the tradition with Brianna. I was hoping, however, that at four o'clock in the afternoon, Shane and I might be alone. The Falls was a very peaceful place to talk, with the sound of the rushing water filling in any awkward silences. Nature's white noise machine.

I walked right up to the edge of the water, feeling the cool mist on my face, and breathed deeply. No fumes. I closed my eyes and listened to the sounds. No cars. It was also about a million times warmer than it would be in Massachusetts at this time of year. I could easily get used to this. Despite the relative warmth, I shivered and Shane pulled me into his chest. I nestled my head against his neck, wishing that we had come here simply for a romantic afternoon, and thinking back to the last time that we'd been at the Falls together.

* * *

THE SUMMER AFTER SENIOR YEAR, and one month before I left for college, our family cat Pickles passed away. We'd had Pickles for as long as I could remember, and he and I had become very good friends. A portly little gentleman, Pickles and I had spent many an afternoon curled up on my bed—me doing my homework, him fast asleep. Sometimes we switched tasks, with Pickles studying various birds on the front lawn, while I snoozed away until dinnertime. Never much of a talker, Pickles was the perfect companion after a long, draining day at school.

The day that I found Pickles—at the ripe old feline age of nineteen—unmoving beneath my bed, I'd fled to the peaceful seclusion of the Falls. Mercifully, there was nobody else around, and I sat quietly sobbing on a bench for a good half an hour. The sound of footsteps had startled me, and I quickly wiped my eyes before turning around.

"You," I said, as Shane came through the trees, water bottle in hand.

"*You*," said Shane. He walked over and joined me on the bench, scrutinizing my face. I turned away. "You okay?"

"Yeah. It's just…. there's been a death in the family."

"Oh," said Shane, immediately losing his casual manner. "I'm so sorry, Caity. Who…who was it?"

"Pickles."

"Oh."

"Don't say *oh*, like it doesn't matter," I snapped.

"That wasn't what I meant," said Shane. "Take it easy. I was just expecting you to say your grandmother or something. Now that I know we're talking pets, I get it. My dog died three years ago. It was devastating."

"Was it really?" I asked, my voice dripping with sarcasm. My grief had stripped away all my patience for humans. Particularly this one.

"Yeah," he said, angling his body toward me and looking me in the eye. "It was."

When I looked back into his eyes, I was surprised to find them full of understanding and sympathy.

"What are you even doing here?" I asked softly, no longer feeling the need for sarcasm. Now more at ease, I looked him up and down, taking notice of his skin which was tanned and glistening with a bit of sweat.

"Just out for a walk," he said, shaking his water bottle. "But enough about me. Tell me about this Pickles."

I sighed and slouched down a bit on the bench. "Pickles was a great friend. A fantastic listener. A connoisseur of fish-flavored pâté."

"He sounds classy."

"He *was* classy. He was the classiest guy in the whole world. And you know what else?"

"What?"

"Pickles *never* asked me why I was so quiet. Pickles *liked* that about me. It wasn't some mystery to him that needed solving. We were kindred spirits." A lump formed again in my throat. "When I was alone in a room with Pickles, I could be alone without *really* being alone. You know? There was no pressure. I could relax and be myself, yet there was still someone there to love. Someone who understood me at my most basic level. Do you know what I mean?"

Shane looked at me curiously, brows furrowed, most likely thinking I'd gone completely off my rocker. Yet, instead of side-stepping his way back into the woods from whence he'd come, he nodded in agreement.

"Anyway," I continued. "How sad is it that the creature I've connected with most in life was a *cat*?"

Shane chuckled. "That's not sad, Caity. And I'm not surprised. In four years of knowing you..." He trailed off.

"What?"

He shrugged. "You're unlike anybody else I know, that's all. And that is to be taken as the highest compliment. You may not be a talker, but when you do"—he paused dramatically to take a sip of water— "it's worth the wait."

He reached over and playfully tugged on a lock of hair that was hanging over my shoulder. Then he added softly, "I felt lucky every time I got to sit next to you on that bus. I'm going to miss that."

"Me, too."

As our eyes locked, thoughts of poor Pickles suddenly took a back seat to other things brewing inside my head.

"Anyway," said Shane, clearing his throat. "Pickles was lucky, too. Even luckier than me, because he got to be with you every day. I would say, he had a pretty good life."

"Thank you," I said, giving him a grateful smile. "And I'm sorry about your dog. I never even knew you had one."

"There are a lot of things you don't know about me, Cook."

"It's a shame we're all out of bus rides," I said, staring sadly into the Falls.

We'd sat there companionably for a while longer, before heading off on our separate ways. But there was a spark between us when we parted that afternoon. A spark that would ignite one month later, and then be put on hold for eight long years.

CHAPTER 19

J pulled myself back to the present and led Shane toward one of the wooden benches. To our right was the evergreen tree upon which visitors to the Falls had hung a variety of Christmas ornaments. It was a Reindeer Falls tradition —come to the waterfall with your true love, and bring along an ornament to place on the tree. Supposedly, doing so would guarantee you a long and happy life together. Many of the ornaments were chipped and faded from the passage of time, and I wondered how those relationships had turned out.

"I need to go back," I said, once we had settled onto the bench. Stating it plainly seemed the only way to do it.

"To your parents' store?" asked Shane. "But we just got here."

"You know what I mean," I said, turning to look at him. Trying to gauge his reaction. "I need to go back to Boston."

He closed his eyes for a moment, then opened them again and stared off toward the top of the Falls. "To pack up your things?"

I sighed. Why was he making this difficult?

"Not to pack up my things," I said. "I've given this a lot of thought, Shane. It just makes the most sense for me to go back...permanently. You *knew* it was a possibility."

He nodded slowly. "Yeah, I knew. I just thought that after..." He trailed off, shaking his head. "What's the big draw, anyway? What is it that's suddenly making this decision so easy for you?"

"A job."

He looked at me, eyebrows raised. "Is it something good? Big museum? University? All-expenses-paid search for the Holy Grail?"

"Houghton Mifflin," I mumbled.

"Hoozi what?"

"Houghton Mifflin," I said again, annunciating each word. "Textbooks."

"Ah, textbooks." He let out a deep sigh. "The same industry you've been in for the past four years, right?"

"Yeah."

"You told me you were bored doing that, didn't you?"

"This is a different company," I said. "A bigger company. It's a great opportunity."

"But still...textbooks?"

The man was relentless. "Yes, still textbooks. That's not the point."

"It sort of is the point, Caity. How'd you get this job? You must have applied for it before you left?"

"Not exactly," I said, shifting uncomfortably on the bench. "My ex-boyfriend, Ben—"

"The one who cheated on you?"

Oh, how I wished that smiling, good-humored Shane would show up soon to replace this demanding doppelganger.

"Yes. The one who cheated on me," I said, through gritted teeth. "But that's not the point. The point is that Ben's father is going to get me a job at Houghton Mifflin. Sort of as...reparations."

"Reparations," mumbled Shane. "There's that word again."

He turned toward me on the bench, looking into my eyes for confirmation that I remembered the significance of the word. Of course, I remembered. There was only one word in the English language that could stop my heart. *Reparations for the past four years,* he had laughed nervously over the phone all those years ago. He'd wanted to take me out for ice cream that night to make up for all the years of teasing me on the bus. He hadn't known that those bus rides were the highlights of my life. I hadn't known that he'd considered himself lucky.

Yes, I needed to go back to Boston, but I also needed him to see that this wasn't the end for us. Not this time.

"Ben and I are over," I said, firmly. "If that's what's bothering you about this, then it shouldn't. Just because his father's getting me a job, it doesn't mean anything. When I go back to Boston, I want to make this work between us, Shane. You and me. Long distance. And, if the interview doesn't go well, and it doesn't look like something I'd even *want,* then I can come back." I took his hand and squeezed it. "I'll come back to you."

If I had some sort of sad delusion that this announcement would send Shane into throes of ecstasy, I couldn't have been more wrong. He pulled his hand out of mine, stood up, and strode several steps away. When he turned around, his face looked tired and full of anguish, an expression I'd never before seen on him. I didn't like it.

"You think you can just come back to me if an interview doesn't go well?" he asked, his face quickly changing from anguish to disbelief. "Caity, I *love* you. There's a reason I'm not seeing anybody. There's a reason that every relationship I've had over the past eight years has fizzled out. It's because nobody I've met has managed to live up to my memories of you. And it's insane, I know. It's insane, because we were so young back then, and we never even—"

"Shane," I interrupted.

"You were my favorite person, Caity," he continued, not letting me speak. "Thanks to whatever sort of bizarre magic you and I conjured up on those bus rides, you got under my skin, and I've never been able to get you out."

"I just—"

"And when you randomly turned up at that concert a few weeks ago," he went on, "it made total sense. It made total sense, because that's how we've always worked. You and I spent half of high school randomly turning up in each other's lives when we needed each other the most. I'd been lonely since I moved back here, Caity, and I'd been thinking about you a lot. I'm working in that high school band room every single day, how could I not? And then suddenly, there you were, staring at my picture in the lobby. Right on schedule. Now you're telling me that I should sit here and wait to find out if I'm the better option than some office job cranking out *textbooks*?"

"That's not what I meant," I said, my voice shaking and my eyes brimming with tears. "I said I wanted us to try long—"

"Long distance, yeah. I know." He raked his hands through his hair, his eyes approaching axe-murderer level intensity. I had no idea I could cause such strong emotions in anybody, let alone Shane Mitchell.

"I don't want long distance," he continued. "If you're going to be with me, then you need to be with me *here*. Maybe it's selfish to tell you to stay, when I'm not willing to pack up and move to Boston. But that's only because I like my life here with the people I've known forever. The people *we've* known forever. You've got roots here, Caity. Boston may be one of the greatest cities in the world, but there's nothing you've told me so far that makes me believe Boston is your home."

Tears were streaming down my cheeks as he closed out his rant. I wanted to tell him that he was right; that Reindeer Falls would always be my home, and that Boston was only a temporary escape that had gone on for too long. But my defense mechanisms were out in full force, telling me that I needed to go back in order to prove to myself that I wasn't a total failure. If I simply let go of the past eight years, it would mean accepting that I'd made no difference to anybody back in Boston. It would mean accepting that I hadn't made any real friends and that I still hadn't found my dream career. It would mean accepting that nobody would even notice I was gone.

I couldn't manage to put any of those feelings into words. At least not into words that Shane, or anybody outside my own head, would understand. Instead of trying to explain, I walked over and placed my hands on his cheeks. I pulled him down to my level and kissed him for a long time. Then I pulled back.

"I love you, too," I said, looking into his eyes. The fact that they were glistening with tears broke my heart, but I continued. "I love you, but I have to go back. For *me*."

The drive back to my parents' house was a silent one. As I stepped out of the car, I paused before closing the door.

"I'll call you," I said.

An unconvincing nod was Shane's only reply. I couldn't blame him for expecting history to repeat itself. I turned and ran up the path to the house, believing that this was, once again, where Shane and I parted ways.

* * *

OVER THE NEXT FEW DAYS, I threw myself into continuing the cleanup of my parents' house—interrupted only by a visit from Michelle, banging on my front door in total crisis mode. She'd also been dealing with unexpected phone calls from an ex-boyfriend, and needed someone to listen. I was so glad that I happened to be back in Reindeer Falls when she needed me. For those few hours that we talked, I was once again struck by the appeal of having my childhood friends close by.

By the end of the week it seemed unlikely that the crew from any of the hoarding television shows would find anything of interest to film. Nate seemed happy and could even be found doing his homework at the kitchen counter from time to time. Home-cooked meals were coming more frequently, and I was confident that Mom and Dad would attempt to stay organized, at least until Nate was out of the house. I felt that I could go back to Boston with at least one part of my life settled. I went online and purchased a plane ticket for after the new year.

When I wasn't cleaning, or having heart-to-hearts with Michelle, I was curled up in bed with Shane's song clutched to my chest, wondering if I was making the biggest mistake of my life. Maybe. Probably. The thing was, it wasn't as if I wanted to break up with him. I loved him and I wanted to try long-distance. It was Shane who was being stubborn. He told me himself that he wasn't willing to move to Boston. Relationships were about compromise, weren't they? If Shane couldn't at least attempt a long-distance relationship, then maybe he didn't love me as much as he thought he did. If this second chance we were handed didn't pan out, it was his fault this time, not mine.

Besides, it was insulting that he assumed it would be so easy for me to pick up and move. Maybe I didn't have many ties to Boston right now, but once I went back, I would finally put in some effort. I would do whatever it took to become part of a social circle again. I'd go to cocktail parties and kickball tournaments, or whatever it was that women in their twenties liked to do together. Not that I particularly *wanted* to do any of those things. A quiet night in with the one person who understood me —that's what I really enjoyed. But I didn't want to be a social failure, either. I didn't want to be someone who could pack up and move to Tennessee, after having lived in a place for eight years, and not even be missed. Because *that*...that was too humiliating to accept.

On the morning of Christmas Eve, I drove to Miss Annabeth's house to bring her a Christmas present. I hadn't yet told her about my Beanie Baby fortune. I had been waiting until I had proof that someone out there was willing to pay thousands of dollars for these things, and now I had it. Claude the crab had sold on eBay that very week. Somebody in Texas was going to be thrilled when they pulled that tie-dyed crustacean out of their stocking on Christmas morning. What Miss Annabeth was going to pull out of her stocking was a six-thousand-dollar check made out to the community center, with the promise of more to come. She wouldn't take my kidney, but she was darn well going to take this. That much I knew.

One more part of my life, settled.

I rang the doorbell and waited patiently for an answer, wishing that I had a way to let myself in. Miss Annabeth shouldn't have to drag herself to the door. I was contemplating peeking underneath the mat for a key, when the door flew open.

"Hello, hello!" said Miss Annabeth, sweeping me inside with a hug and a kiss. She was wearing a gold Christmas wreath brooch on the lapel of her red cardigan sweater, with matching gold earrings. She looked rested, and had even put on a bit of makeup. Having her girls back in town seemed to have worked wonders on her health.

My heart lifting, I followed her inside the house. I knew if there was one person who would give me an honest, wise, and relatively unbiased opinion, it was Miss Annabeth. Even though I was always the quiet one, I suddenly felt a million things to say bubbling up inside of me.

CHAPTER 20

*B*ut, first things were first.

I sat down on the couch next to Miss Annabeth and looked around the living room. Much like my parents' house, Miss Annabeth's house had also undergone a huge improvement over the past few weeks. The three of us had been taking turns stopping by to help with the housekeeping, so there were no more dirty dishes or baskets of unfolded laundry lying around. We'd also spent an evening watching *It's a Wonderful Life* and decorating the tree that Shane had so kindly had delivered. It stood cheerfully in the corner of the living room, smelling like the holidays, and already twinkling. Burl Ives was curled up underneath the tree, peacefully asleep. I smiled and handed Miss Annabeth the small gift bag I had been carrying.

"This is for you. Merry Christmas."

"You didn't have to do that," she said. She reached into the bag and pulled out a plain brown Beanie Baby bear with a red bow around its neck. "Oh, he's adorable."

"He's worthless," I said.

"It's the thought that counts, dear."

I laughed. "No, I mean, *this* one is worthless. It's symbolic.

148

Open the envelope." I pointed excitedly at the envelope that was secured in the worthless bear's arms.

With a curious smile, Miss Annabeth tore open the envelope and stared at the check. She put one hand over her mouth. "Oh *my*. Six thousand dollars? What is this about, Caity?" She lowered the check and looked at me in shock.

"I sold a kidney," I deadpanned. "You wouldn't take it, so I found someone who would." I rubbed my abdomen as the poor woman stared at me, eyes wide.

"*Caity!*"

"Bad joke!" I held my hands up before she could get mad. Well, madder.

She rolled her eyes and swatted me gently on the arm. "The *truth*, please."

"The truth is that I found bags full of mint condition Beanie Babies in my closet that are worth thousands of dollars. That check is the first of many, and I'm donating *all* of them to the community center."

"But"—Miss Annabeth raised her hand in protest. I shushed her.

"No buts. This is my Christmas present to you. I believe I owe you quite a few since I've been gone. Consider it...reparations." The word sent a flutter through my stomach that I tried to squash down. It was just a word, for Pete's sake. Shane didn't own the rights to it.

"Oh, Caity." She put her arms around me and pulled me into a hug. "You don't owe me anything. But all the same...*thank you*."

"You're very welcome." I closed my eyes and held on tightly, the idea of losing this sweet woman suddenly swallowing me up with grief. A sob escaped me and Miss Annabeth gently stroked my hair.

"It's going to be okay," she said. "I promise. Remember what you told me? If there's one place destined for a Christmas miracle, it's a town called Reindeer Falls."

"But what if there's a town out there called Christmas Falls?" I asked, a small smile breaking through my tears.

Miss Annabeth laughed. "Well, then. I guess we're screwed."

It felt good to laugh, and after a few moments, she gently released me from her arms and walked over to the piano. There was a small holiday bag sitting by the music stand.

"I have a little something for you, as well," she said. "It's not much. Just something I saw at the pharmacy when I was picking up my medication. Us old people do that sort of thing quite a bit. Milton Picklebarrel and I are total BFFs." With a dramatic roll of her eyes, she handed me the bag along with a tissue.

I smiled and wiped away my tears. Inside the gift bag, nestled in a tuft of tissue paper, was a red, heart-shaped suncatcher. In the center hung two silver eighth notes dotted with crystals.

"It's beautiful," I breathed, holding it up toward the window. I flipped over the tag that was hanging from the hook and read what it said. *Love Notes. Handmade in Reindeer Falls.* She had found this at the pharmacy? I pictured the pharmacy back in Harvard Square, full of mass-produced Boston themed trinkets. I clasped it to my chest. "I love it. Thank you."

"You're welcome, dear. I was thinking it might look good on the ornament tree by the Falls. Perhaps you and Mr. Mitchell could make a little visit?"

With a sigh, I put the ornament gently back into the bag.

"Uh, oh," she said. "What happened?"

"Do you mind?" I motioned to the couch.

"Not at all."

I stretched out lengthwise on the couch while Miss Annabeth took a seat in the wingback chair opposite. Therapist and patient, assuming their positions. My head had barely hit the pillow when the words started pouring out of me. I told her everything, starting from the night before I had left for Harvard, up until my most recent argument with Shane at the Falls. When I finished talking, I felt drained. Talking often did that to me. But I also felt quite a bit lighter. Everything I'd been carrying around with me for the past eight years had been dumped out on the front lawn, like Mom and Dad's antiques, ready to be analyzed and sorted. Ready for somebody to tell me what I should do with them. Throw away...or keep?

"That's quite a story," said Miss Annabeth.

"No kidding," I said, staring up at the ceiling, finding pictures in the plaster swirls.

"Tell me," she continued. "If money were no object, and you could spend your days doing anything in the world, what would you do?"

I blinked up at the ceiling in silence until the pictures faded away. Then I turned my head toward Miss Annabeth.

"I suppose I would start playing the piano more," I said. "I'd try to get really good again. Maybe give free lessons to kids?"

"That's lovely, dear. But it would also leave a lot of free time. What else?"

I stared at the ceiling again until an image of Mom and Dad's barn came into my mind and I felt a ping of excitement.

"Antiques," I said. "I would go antiquing. I'd seek out and rescue pieces of history, and I'd organize the heck out of my parents' barn. I'd find good homes for all those treasures, before they were lost. I would do it all for free if I could."

"Right there," said Miss Annabeth. "That's your passion, Caity. Not textbooks. I know you feel with a Harvard education you should be seeking out some big, fancy career in a skyscraper in the city"—she made big, fancy skyscraper motions with her hands— "but there's no shame in doing what you love. With your brains, and your parents' antique shop, you could do great things right here in Reindeer Falls. The town would be lucky to have you back."

"But, Miss Annabeth," I said, struggling to fight back a fresh wave of tears. "How do I get past the fact that I lived somewhere for eight years and have nothing to show for it?"

"What are you talking about?"

"I mean that hardly anybody in Boston knows I exist! You know that it's always been hard for me to make friends. I'm quiet, and I'm introverted, and the older I get...well, it doesn't really seem to get any easier to connect with people. I could never go back to Boston and it wouldn't make an ounce of difference to anybody."

"So what?"

"What do you mean *so what?*" I said, sitting up. "It's depressing! That's *what.* I don't want to be the kind of person who barely existed!"

"You think you barely exist?" asked Miss Annabeth, her face darkening. "You listen to me. Yes, you're quiet. And yes, you're introverted. But those things make you who you are. And who you are is one of the most funny, talented, and caring people I've ever met—with a group of friends who would do anything for you. Have you forgotten about them?"

"No," I muttered.

"I hope not. Maybe you've lost touch over the years, but that bracelet ritual was binding. It may sound silly, but I believe in it. Don't make those girls out to be some meaningless memory from your past. Those girls love you, Caity. *I* love you. And so do your parents, and your brother, and Shane. That boy was in love with you all the way through high school. I don't know how you possibly missed it."

She paused for breath, while I stared at her, dumbstruck. When she was ready, she started again.

"Don't you *dare* tell me that you barely exist. You girls mean the world to me. Who cares if a million strangers in Boston don't know anything about you? Caitlin Cook doesn't open up to millions of strangers. That's not her way, and that's a *good* thing. You open up to the select few who deserve you. The lucky ones. And lo and behold, the lucky ones just happen to live in this middle-of-nowhere town in Tennessee. If you think you need to run back to Boston in order to prove something to yourself, then you need to open your eyes. All the proof of your worth is right here. Use that big brain of yours, Caitlin Marie Cook. Before it's too late."

I closed my gaping jaw. I'd never heard such blunt words come out of Miss Annabeth's normally reserved mouth. Well, maybe that time the roof collapsed at the community center. Still, I felt as if I'd been slapped in the face. Which was, apparently, exactly what I needed. With shaking hands, I gripped the edge of the couch, my eyes darting around the room.

"You brilliant old woman," I said, standing up and throwing my arms around her neck. "I love you. You know that, right?"

"Yes, of course," she said, with a bewildered blink.

"Good." I kissed her on top of her head, grabbed the gift bag with the ornament, and ran out the front door. "I'll see you soon!"

I jumped into Dad's Harvester, turned on the engine, and dialed Nate's cell phone. It rang about a billion times.

"Pick up, pick up, pick up," I muttered to myself.

"Hello?" he answered, still sounding half asleep.

"It's me!" I said. "Wake up. I need your help!"

"What *time* is it?"

"It's eleven o'clock in the morning. *Get out of bed!*"

"Who *is* this?"

I pulled the phone away from my ear and banged it against my forehead.

"Nate," I said, calmly, the phone back against my ear. "It's your sister. Your loving sister. And she needs a favor."

"I already told you, I'm never putting that reindeer suit on again. Did I tell you that they hung that newspaper photo on the school bulletin board?"

"It's not that," I said, biting my lip and trying not to laugh. Poor Nate. "I need you to call your friends. I don't care if they're asleep. Call them. Trumpet players. Drummers. Flute players. Call everybody! Tell them to clear their schedules for tonight."

"It's Christmas Eve, Caitlin."

"I *know* that, Nathan. This will take, like, thirty minutes of their time."

"Thirty minutes?"

"Okay, an hour. Tops. Tell them it's for Mr. Mitchell." There was silence on the other end. "Hello? You still there?" If he'd gone back to sleep, I was going to kill him.

"You should've said that in the first place," said Nate. "Whatever you're up to, I'm in. But no more favors until next Christmas."

"Deal," I said, bouncing up and down in my seat. "Thank you, Nate."

I hung up with my brother and called Shane, keeping the conversation short.

"Will you be home tonight at six?" I asked.

"Uh, yeah," he said. "Look, I'm glad you called. I—"

Without letting him finish, I hung up and took off toward home.

CHAPTER 21

"Okay," I said, checking the time on my phone, my stomach jittery with nerves. And three cups of coffee from Holly's. But mostly nerves. "We've got seven minutes. Those lights turn on automatically at six o'clock. I want us out front and ready to go when that happens. Let's move it, people!"

I was standing before a group of twenty-two teenagers in marching band uniforms. My little brother had really come through. He'd managed to scrape up an entire drum line, some trumpets and saxophones, several woodwinds, and four girls twirling red and white flags, which I hadn't even requested. Nate just thought they would be a nice touch. I'd assembled everybody one street over from Shane's house under the cover of darkness —which sounds exciting and mysterious, but actually resulted in a bunch of groping, giggling teenagers—and I was attempting to get everybody into some sort of order. Earlier in the afternoon, I'd driven around town distributing sheet music to all the kids on Nate's list, but we'd had no chance to actually rehearse as a group. I couldn't even let anybody warm-up their instruments without alerting the entire neighborhood to what was going on outside. I was also counting on the solar flare-like glow of

Shane's Christmas lights to allow everybody to read their parts in the dark.

As Miss Annabeth said, it's the thought that counts.

"Band ten hut!" I hissed, and everybody snapped to attention. My stomach was queasy with dorkiness. It had been years since I'd heard, let alone spoken, a marching band command. But it came back to me as if no time had passed at all, and it seemed to do the trick. All the giggling and groping immediately ceased. I turned and started leading the group down the side of the road—green Halloween glow stick in hand—praying that nobody got hit by a car on my account. That would probably be the worst of all possible outcomes. The second worst of all possible outcomes would be if Shane slammed the door in my face.

We arrived safely outside the house and assembled into a large semi-circle on the front lawn. There were several lights on inside the house, including one upstairs, where—if I remembered correctly—Mr. Mitchell's study was located. Weird. I didn't have much time to contemplate it, though, as I looked at my phone and watched the timer counting down.

Three...two...one...

I blinked several times as the lights came on, the sheer amount of them bringing a smile to my face. I spun around and blew three times into my whistle, sending the band into the slow opening notes of "All I Want for Christmas Is You." It was a bit rough around the edges, and the horns were sort of out of tune due to the cold weather, but the kids were certainly giving it their all. As they broke into the rollicking first verse, I gave them a big thumbs-up and turned back around to face the house. I held my breath until the front door opened and out stepped Shane.

And behind him, his parents.

Right.

That would explain the light on in the study. I'd forgotten that Shane's parents were flying in from Florida for the holidays—a small detail that might make things a bit awkward. Although,

Shane's parents probably didn't even remember me from high school. This little performance would either leave a lasting, and positive, first impression, or it would make me appear totally desperate and strange. Whatever. Shane's parents were the least of my worries right now.

My main worry was standing there on the doorstep, looking totally bewildered and adorable. He turned around, shook his head, and said something to his parents. His father nodded. His mother smiled and clasped her hands against her chest, probably thinking this sort of thing was a normal occurrence for a band director.

Shane turned back to us, and when his eyes finally found me, he left his parents behind and jogged across the lawn. I hadn't seen him in days, and I melted at the sight of him standing there in front of me, blue eyes questioning what in the world was going on. No matter how this evening turned out, at least he would know that this time I'd come back. And in the loudest way possible.

"What is this?" he asked, glancing behind me, a huge smile on his face. "Those are my kids! You hijacked my kids?"

"They wouldn't have done this for anybody but you," I said, smiling up at him.

We turned toward the band and listened to the rest of the song—flags twirling, cymbals crashing, trumpets wailing. By the time they reached the end, I was more than ready to talk to Shane. I turned to him, took a deep breath, and—

They started up the song again.

"Oh," I said, suddenly remembering what I had to do. "Sorry. Hang on." When the band reached the end of the next verse, I made a dramatic cut-off gesture with my arms.

The band went silent.

"That's better," I said, turning and looking up at Shane, shivering slightly. The temperature was still dropping and it felt like snow. I suddenly wanted nothing more than to go into the house and curl up by the fire. I didn't even care if Mr. and Mrs. Mitchell were home, or if they thought I was desperate and strange. I just wanted to be done with the drama and get on with the happily ever after. Still, Shane deserved this grand gesture, and it wasn't quite finished yet.

"Merry Christmas Eve," he said. "This is...amazing."

"Consider it reparations," I said softly. "Reparations for being so incredibly blind all these years. Look, Shane, I came here tonight because—"

"I want to try long distance," he blurted out, cutting me off before I could finish.

"What?"

"I tried to tell you earlier, but you hung up on me. If long distance is the only way we can be together, then of course I'll try it. I was being a selfish idiot when I said that I wouldn't. And if it doesn't work out, then I'll move to Boston. I just—"

I reached out and put one hand on his chest. "Please. Stop."

He stiffened, bracing for the bad news. *Come on, Shane,* I thought. *Who brings a marching band to bear bad news?* The thought made me smile, and I saw the relief that my smile brought to his face. That's when I realized that it had always been that way. During all of our little moments throughout the years, his smile and his presence had always comforted me. And mine had done the same for him.

"I love you," I said, putting my other hand on his chest. "I came here tonight to tell you that I'm staying in Reindeer Falls."

"But I thought you wanted to go back to Boston?" he asked slowly. "I don't want you giving up on your dreams because of me, Caity. If you want to live in Boston, then you should. We'll make it work."

"Boston isn't my dream," I said, shaking my head. "Boston was for college, and some job experience, and some really good sports teams." Shane crinkled his nose, and I laughed. "But my dreams are *here*. My dreams are about that antique shop, and getting back into music, and being with my true friends and my family. My dreams are about finally getting to be with you. It's what I've been dreaming about ever since I left." I playfully kicked at the toe of his sneaker. "I thought I needed to go back to Boston in order to prove something to myself. I felt like some sort of massive failure for having lived somewhere for so long without managing to have anything to go back to. Does that make sense? I felt like there was something seriously wrong with me."

"Oh, Caity," he sighed, slipping his arms around me and speaking into the top of my head. "Who cares if a million strangers in some big city don't know anything about you? That's not your way."

"A wise old lady told me the same thing this morning."

"Well, it's true. I used to see you at school, laughing with those girls you'd known forever, but you never talked to me. You were always such a mystery. When I finally got you alone on those bus rides, I got to see inside that head of yours...and I was in love. It suddenly didn't matter to me *why* you were quiet. It was just who you were. The best thing in the world."

I lifted my head and kissed him for a long time after that, not caring that his parents, and my brother, and half of a high school marching band were watching. Just sinking into the warmth of his body, letting his words wash away the last of my self-doubts. Silently rejoicing that Shane was mine at last, and that I was never going to let him go. Although...I didn't need to rejoice in *total* silence.

"Hang on," I whispered, taking a step back. I turned around and put the whistle between my lips. As I blew four times to signal the start of "Joy to the World," fluffy flakes of snow started falling from the sky, and a round of applause and whistles came from the front steps of the house. I turned and waved to Shane's parents.

"You know," I said, dropping my whistle and putting my arms back around Shane's neck, "I'm going to need someone to come up to Boston and help me move. We could do some sightseeing. You could finally buy me that bookstore beer."

Shane laughed. "Sounds like a plan."

"And, since we'll have a nice long drive back to Tennessee together, I found a little something to pass the time."

"Oh, yeah?"

I reached inside my coat and pulled out the black and white chevron notebook with the pink spiral binding. I opened it to the first page.

"First question. Have you ever..." I stood on my tiptoes and whispered the rest of it into his ear. Shane burst out laughing and pulled me closer, not answering the question. We never answered the questions.

Instead, we stood on the lawn as the snow came down, wrapped up in each other's arms, and listening to the music. I was happy, and I was home. I was right back where I'd started, in a little town called Reindeer Falls.

The lights twinkled, and the band played on.

EPILOGUE

I set my alarm for bright and early on Christmas morning, jumped out of bed, and banged on Nate's door until he dragged himself into the hall.

"Do you ever consider what time it is?" he asked. "Like, ever?"

"It's Christmas morning, dope! Nobody sleeps in on Christmas morning! Besides, I think I smell cinnamon buns."

Nate's eyes opened slightly wider as he sniffed the air like a basset hound and took off down the stairs. We followed the smell into the warm kitchen where Mom and Dad were already awake and drinking coffee—Mom in her ratty, old pink bathrobe, and Dad in his red flannel pajamas. Christmas music played softly from the antique radio by the stove.

"Merry Christmas!" I said, giving them each a kiss on the cheek.

"Merry Christmas, love," said Mom. "We weren't expecting you two up so early!"

I ignored the dirty look Nate gave me as I cut a cinnamon bun out of the pan on the stove, and poured myself some coffee.

"I was just too excited to sleep," I said. And it was true. Between everything that had happened last night with Shane, and my nerves over today's upcoming show, I'd barely slept at all. I'd even been awake long enough to hear Dad curse as he tripped over something in the living room while trying to sneak presents under the tree.

"You know, I think I heard Santa last night," I said, as the four of us made our way into the living room to exchange gifts. "He sounded sort of...angry." I bit back a laugh as Dad's face slowly turned pink.

"Don't know what you mean," he said, glancing anxiously at Mom. "Didn't hear a thing."

"Mm hmm," I mumbled, giving him a playful nudge as he busied himself with the fireplace.

Mom opened her presents first—a lovely antique ring from Dad (which he adamantly denied being part of his haul from Esther Adams' estate sale), and the sweatshirt and bathrobe that Nate and I had picked out. Dad loved his eBay gift card from Mom, and the new tools Nate and I had selected at Sears. After I'd come into my Beanie Baby fortune, I'd also gone out and bought a few additional gifts for my family. A unique vintage handbag for Mom. Floormats for the Harvester for Dad. For Nate, I'd had the *Reindeer Falls Gazette's* photograph of the three of us dressed as Santa, Mrs. Claus, and Clip-Clop enlarged and framed. I burst out laughing when I opened Nate's present to me —the photograph he'd found in Shane's office drawer, framed.

"How did you get this?" I asked, wiping tears from my eyes. There I was, seated on the ground with my flute in my lap. Shane stood behind me, goofily pretending to play the drums on my head, and I felt butterflies in my stomach at the thought of seeing him again in a few hours.

"I may have gone through Mr. M's drawer...one last time," he said, rubbing the back of his neck. "I'd, um, I'd keep that photo under the radar if I were you."

"Will do," I laughed. "And thank you."

The last gift to be opened was for me, from Mom and Dad. I

pulled the ribbon off a tiny silver box, to find my very own key to Christmas Past nestled inside.

"I love it," I said, taking it out and clasping it to my chest. Even the key to the shop looked like an antique. I couldn't wait to slip it onto my keyring.

"It's a real family business now," said Mom, smiling warmly and squeezing Dad's hand. They both looked ridiculously happy.

It was the best Christmas morning I'd had in a long time, and before I knew it, I was showered and dressed and ready to drive to the community center for the Christmas show. Even though I'd practiced as much as I possibly could, I was still filled with nerves as I pulled on my coat and grabbed the sheet music from the piano.

"We're all so excited to hear you play again," said Mom, giving my arm a squeeze as we walked outside to the car. "We're all so proud of you, Caity."

"Just don't mess up," said Nate, giving me a gentle shove as he scooted past me down the walk.

We parked alongside the town square, walking past Santa's Landing Strip before heading to the community center. We didn't always get snow for Christmas in Tennessee, so I wasn't surprised to find that some overly excited soul had come out here early to make reindeer prints and sleigh tracks in the snow. Several children ran excitedly around, looking for any other evidence Santa may have left behind. I wondered who it had been. Giles Wilson? Rudy Clemson? I turned around and gave the statue of Clip-Clop a wink, just in case.

We walked across the town square and into the community center, finding it warm, inviting, and alive with activity, just like in the old days. I looked around and smiled at all the faces that I recognized, and at all the things that hadn't changed. Brightly covered folding tables had been pushed up against the wall, laid out with familiar holiday cookies from Holly's and cups of hot chocolate with candy cane stirrers. Wooden folding chairs had been set up in long rows in front of the stage, with red velvet bows attached to the ones reserved for special guests. There was a seat in the center of the front row that I knew had to have been saved for Miss Annabeth, who I still hadn't seen yet.

I left Mom, Dad, and Nate in their seats, and walked backstage to look for Miss Annabeth and my friends. I spotted her immediately, looking tired but undoubtedly happy. The wish that she had made was actually coming true—all of her girls were back in Reindeer Falls and about to perform for her again. It was going to be beautiful… just as long as I didn't mess up. Thanks, Nate.

I walked over and gave her a hug.

"I heard that something quite interesting happened last night," said Miss Annabeth, pulling away and looking questioningly up into my eyes.

"It may have," I said, fighting back the huge smile that threatened to come out every time I thought of Shane. She was clearly waiting for me to elaborate, but I just couldn't find the words.

"Don't worry," she said, shaking her head. "I'll find out the juicy details later, from Dottie. Just tell me this…are you happy?"

"Yes," I said. "Very."

"Good." Her eyes suddenly shifted to someone behind me, and she smiled. I turned around to find Shane standing there in a red button-up shirt and his surfing Santa Claus necktie.

"Cool tie," I said, stepping closer and poking at the center of it, setting off that tinny rendition of "Deck the Halls."

"Thanks."

I didn't let go of the tie as he leaned down to kiss me, forgetting for a moment that Miss Annabeth was standing right there. After last night's marching band incident, I seemed to be getting more comfortable with public displays of affection. We were interrupted much too soon by a loud wolf whistle. I pulled away to find both Emma and Michelle standing there, smiling, and nodding at us in approval.

"I knew it," was all Emma said, before wrapping me in a hug and shaking me back and forth.

"You're a wild and crazy girl," said Michelle, giving me a hug once Emma had let me go. "It's always the—"

"Don't you dare say it," I interrupted, giving her a warning glare.

"*Redheads*," said Michelle, holding her hands up in front of her. "It's always the redheads."

Soon we were all chatting happily away with Miss Annabeth. Emma, who had taken that job in the bookstore after all, told us that she was looking into finally going to college. Michelle told us that after eight years in California, she'd also decided to move home to Reindeer Falls in order to be closer to her grandparents. As I looked around at my friends, I felt so blessed to have been given this second chance at reconnecting with them, and so excited for what the future held. My only wish was that Miss Annabeth be healthy enough to witness our friendships growing once again.

At least the community center seemed to be in decent shape. While I'd been busy selling off my Beanie Babies, Emma had purchased a used copy of *Harry Potter and the Sorcerer's Stone* to read on her lunch break. What she hadn't known—until I happened to pick it up and flip open the cover—was that it was a first edition worth a few thousand dollars. Michelle did her part by happily selling off a few pieces of expensive jewelry that had been gifts from her ex-boyfriend.

Miss Annabeth's eyes grew wider with each check she was handed, and when we added up the total, it seemed to be enough to keep the community center open for at least one more year. After that, we would have to figure out something else. But at least we were all going to be here, facing the future together.

"Hey, what's that sound?" asked Shane. We all quieted down and listened.

"Miss Annabeth, I think that's you," said Emma.

Several checks fell out of Miss Annabeth's hand as she reached into her pants pocket and pulled out the pager from the hospital. She looked around, questioningly, at each of us.

"If this means what I think—"

"Go!" We all shouted. "Call them back!"

With shaking hands, she took the cell phone Michelle offered and dialed the number. We waited with bated breath while she said frustratingly vague things like "yes" and "I understand." Finally, she hung up, and turned to us with a disbelieving smile and eyes full of tears.

"They've found me a match," she said. "They've scheduled me for surgery tomorrow morning."

With a cheer, we all swooped in to hug her.

"Looks like we got that Christmas miracle," I whispered.

"Yes, we did," she whispered back.

As the show began, Shane went out to join my family in the audience, and Miss Annabeth walked onstage to speak. Another cheer went through the crowd as she told the entire town her good news.

Emma, Michelle, and I watched each of the performances from the wings. There were the elementary school kids singing "Jingle Bell Rock," and Dottie Cross doing her annual dramatic reading of *How the Grinch Stole Christmas.* A group of high school students did a hip-hop dance routine to an interesting remix of "Rudolph the Red-Nosed Reindeer" that made poor Milton Picklebarrel—seated in the front row—look a bit scandalized.

And then, suddenly, it was our turn. The final act of the show. With shaking hands, I took my place at the piano, taking comfort in all the familiar scratches and scuffs. I glanced out into the audience at Shane, my parents, and Nate. At this whole town I hadn't even realized I had missed. I took a deep breath as Emma and Michelle climbed onto their stools and picked up their microphones.

Just don't mess up. Nate's annoying words echoed again in my head. But it was okay this time, because I knew now that I wasn't going to mess this up. Not this song, not this love, not anything about this second chance I'd been so graciously given. Miss Annabeth was going to make the most out of the second chance she'd been given, and I planned to follow in her remarkable footsteps.

My nerves calmed, and I began to play.

The End

ACKNOWLEDGMENTS

Thank you to Craig DeMelo for
"A Rose on Fire"

Please visit him on iTunes and www.thewhiskeypoet.com

Turn the page for a preview of Michelle's story

Merry Little Love Story
in
Reindeer Falls

Shop Now on Amazon

MERRY LITTLE LOVE STORY

Ten years ago, at the Falls…

I tried to look cool, slipping our ornament onto a branch of the old evergreen tree. We'd bought the ornament—a tiny wooden cuckoo clock, with a yellow bird at the top and two golden pine cones dangling from chains at the bottom—for a whopping $1.99 at Nick's General Store, since it was the week after Christmas and everything had been slashed to half-price. Legend had it, hanging an ornament from this particular tree by the Falls would guarantee you and your loved one a long and happy life together. Of course, we all knew it was just a silly tradition, started by the people of Reindeer Falls who'd grown up before cell phones and video games, back when hanging up an ornament was the most exciting thing they'd do all week.

Still, even those dull old-timey people couldn't possibly have believed it would actually work. I mean, it was just a tree, and trees didn't have magical powers. This tree didn't even have a wise, old face carved into it like the cool one at Clemson's Christmas Tree Farm (and Rudy Clemson never once claimed that *his* tree could perform miracles). No, the Reindeer Falls ornament tree was simply another one of our kooky small-town traditions, which just happened to be the sort of thing that Ryan Cross was crazy about.

I'd protested coming here at all—mostly out of fear that someone from school might see me—but Ryan had insisted. What did he care? He didn't have any friends around here. *Let's do it,* he'd said. *Just in case.* I couldn't really argue with that. I also couldn't argue with that sparkle in his eyes. Those deep brown eyes of his sparkled the entire time he was in Reindeer Falls, which was for just one week out of the year.

Ryan had been coming to Reindeer Falls ever since he was old enough to board an airplane alone. At age six, on the day after Christmas, his parents put him on a plane from Boston to Tennessee to visit his great-aunt Dottie, while they took off to the Bahamas for an adults-only getaway. When Ryan returned home in one piece, his parents had dubbed it an annual tradition. The Cross family was involved in real estate development—they owned apartment complexes all across the Northeast—and were rolling in money, which was why they got away with doing weirdo things like putting their six-year-old son on a plane all by himself. They didn't pay a heck of a lot of attention to him the rest of the year, either.

Luckily for me, Dottie was my next-door neighbor, and Ryan was a pretty decent follow-up to Santa Claus. That first year, he'd arrived in a limousine from the airport with a pile of suitcases, filled with a zillion new toys and video games.

"This is so lame," I said, brushing my dark bangs out of my eyes and stepping back from the tree. At least I wasn't holding onto the ornament anymore. If anyone from school showed up now, I could just pretend that we'd come up to the Falls to drink. Not that we drank, unless you counted all the hot chocolates we ordered from Holly's.

"It is not lame," said Ryan softly, nudging me with his elbow. "You know I don't have this sort of thing back home."

I looked up at his eyes to catch that sparkle. I smiled and let him enjoy his moment. Ryan had nearly everything in the world back home; everything except kooky small-town traditions, and he couldn't get enough of them.

As we stood there, I looked around at some of the other ornaments that had been left on the tree over the years—snowflakes, gingerbread houses, lots and lots of reindeer. There was an elf ornament halfway up that had that deranged, 1960s look to it. For all I knew, that elf had been left by a much younger Gran and Gramps; they were big believers in the power of the ornament tree. Gramps had actually hung an ornament with a different girl, back before he met Gran. When Gran found out, she dragged Gramps down to the Falls, made him identify the ornament, and then—instead of throwing it in the trash or burning it, like a normal jealous girlfriend—she'd donated it to the church thrift shop. Gotta love my Gran. After that, they hung up an ornament of their own and were married two months later.

"So," I said, turning toward Ryan and stepping a bit closer. He put his hands on my waist and I rested mine on the front of his coat. "Another year."

"Another year," he repeated wistfully.

"You know, this time next year we'll both be in college," I said. "Maybe you won't even *want* to come down here anymore."

Here's the thing. I wasn't an idiot. I knew that people who only saw each other for one week out of an entire year didn't usually end up together forever. At some point between January and December, they'd meet other people. They'd move on. Ryan and I had even made a pact back when we were fifteen, and had shared our first kiss at midnight on New Year's Eve. We'd agreed that if we were both still single the following year, we would pick up right where we'd left off; but if either of us was dating someone else, we'd go back to being friends. So far, we'd both remained unattached.

"I will never not want to come down here," said Ryan, his eyes sparkling as he glanced at the Falls. He pulled me in closer. "Unless, of course, you meet some hot Smoky Mountain guy right after I get on the plane tomorrow."

"I wouldn't worry," I said, rolling my eyes.

I knew every guy my age in this town, and nobody had ever compared to Ryan. It wasn't that we had a ton in common, exactly. Ryan was this worldly rich kid from Boston who turned into Buddy the Elf whenever he was in Reindeer Falls. Me? I'd been raised by my grandparents since I was six, when my mother took off to Arizona with her new boyfriend, one week before Christmas. I never even met my dad, and I'd certainly never left the state of Tennessee. Even so, Ryan and I always had exactly what the other needed.

He'd come into my life just a week after my mother had left— a tiny ray of sunshine in the middle of the storm. Ryan's parents deserted him *every* year, the moment Christmas was over, while Dottie, Gran, Gramps, and I welcomed him to Reindeer Falls with open arms. The two of us had looked forward to this week together for nearly our entire lives.

I stepped away from the tree, pulling Ryan along with me to one of the wooden benches. It was late afternoon on New Year's Eve, which was always our last night together. New Year's Eve being our last night together was tradition, like fireworks and Dick Clark. Only, Ryan going home was anything but a rockin' good time. Ryan going home was a knife to my heart. Not that there was anything to be done about it. We were only seventeen, and a long-distance relationship just wasn't realistic.

"What time is the party again?" asked Ryan.

"Seven." The town always held a New Year's Eve party for teenagers over at the community center. There would be plenty of food, music, and dancing, but I didn't particularly want to go. Why celebrate the coming of a new year when all I wanted was to stretch out the last week of December into infinity? "We don't have to go, you know? Gran and Gramps go to bed early. We could hang out at my house." I looked up at him and waggled my eyebrows.

"But the party's a tradition," he said, as I knew he would. I'd probably have been worried about him if he hadn't turned me down. "We can't just skip out on a tradition. Not *here*. Not on the last night of the year."

"Okay, okay," I said. It wasn't easy competing with an entire town for Ryan's affection. "It's just been a long month, you know? If I have to hear 'Holly Jolly Christmas' one more time, or sing at that Christmas show one more year…"

Ryan chuckled. "One of these years I'm going to get down here *before* Christmas, so I don't keep missing out on all the good stuff."

I snorted. "Right. You only get to go to fancy holiday parties, have your family's Christmas tree photographed for magazines, get pretty much *any* gift that you want…" I counted each surreal item off on my fingers. "You have plenty of Christmas magic back home. Trust me."

"True," said Ryan, taking my hand and interlacing our fingers. "But it's not the same. All those things take is money. Which works out well for my parents, because they don't have to put any thought into what they get me. But down here, it's different. It's like…*real*, you know? It's in the air. You can't bottle it, Chelle."

Amused, I looked up and studied his face, trying to imagine the last week of December without him here. What did everyone else look forward to after the excitement of Christmas had passed? I had no idea. I leaned forward and pressed my lips to his cheek, my chest aching at the thought that I could lose him to someone else at any point over the next twelve months. Would I even see it coming?

At some point over the last few years, I'd fallen in love with Ryan Cross, Rich Kid from Boston. One week together or fifty-two, it hadn't mattered in the least. I'd never admitted my feelings to him, but I assumed that he felt the same. I assumed that he loved me just as much as he loved this town, and hopefully a bit more. But saying it out loud would only complicate things. The two of us were blessed with this one week, for however long it lasted. And maybe, once we were older—perhaps by the power of the magical ornament tree—we would get to be together for real. Maybe those old-timey people had it right.

"We'd better get back," I said, placing the back of my hand against his cheek, where my lips had been. "It's getting cold."

Hand in hand we walked away from the Falls. Magical ornament tree or not, I had faith that we'd be back here again next year.

Shop Now at Amazon!

OTHER BOOKS BY BETH LABONTE

The Summer Series:
Summer at Sea
Summer at Sunset
Summer Baby

Holiday Sweet Romance:
Love Notes in Reindeer Falls
Merry Little Love Story in Reindeer Falls

Autumnboro Sweet Romance:
Pumpkin Everything
Maple Sugar Crush

More:
Down, Then Up: A Novella

You can also find Beth here:
Facebook
www.bethlabonte.com

Made in the USA
Las Vegas, NV
28 November 2023

81708720R00111